A. M. Donelan

Flora Adair

Love works wonders - Vol. 2

A. M. Donelan

Flora Adair
Love works wonders - Vol. 2

ISBN/EAN: 9783337272746

Printed in Europe, USA, Canada, Australia, Japan

Cover: Foto ©Andreas Hilbeck / pixelio.de

More available books at **www.hansebooks.com**

FLORA ADAIR;

OR,

Love works Wonders.

BY A. M. DONELAN.

"IN FUNICULIS ADAM TRAHAM EOS, IN VINCULIS CHARITATIS."
Osee xi. 4.

IN TWO VOLUMES.
VOL. II.

LONDON:
CHAPMAN AND HALL, 193, PICCADILLY.
1867.

FLORA ADAIR.

CHAPTER I.

WOULD she have said so had she known that, although Mr. Earnscliffe *was* in Venice, all his thoughts were occupied about her?

In proportion as he had been elated and happy with her, so did the next morning find him depressed and sad. He had given himself up completely to the enjoyment of that starlight walk. How pleasant he found it to watch the movements of Flora's little slight figure as she walked by his side, and every now and then to have some thought or feeling which he expressed responded to by a look from her soft eyes. But even as he thought over it all he said to himself, " Yes, it was very delightful ; but will any good come of it ? I knew such an evening long ago ; then, too, I walked with one whom I loved and trusted, and she brought me only misery. Life and hope and faith have been blighted by her. Is it not

worse than folly, then, to believe in a woman
again ? . . . ."

For the last few days he had cast all doubt
from him. He only thought of how Flora had
acted towards Mr. Lyne ; of how true she had been
to him ; so true that not even an unjust accusation
could wring from her a word implying that he
had proposed for her. But now came the reaction. It was not all at once that Mr. Earnscliffe
could divest himself fully of that distrust of
women which for years had been so rooted in his
mind. Then Mary Elton's words and his own
dream forced themselves painfully upon him, and
sounded like a warning which said, " Stop, before
it is too late." " But perhaps it is already too
late," he thought. " Could I forget her even
now ? Have I ever forgotten her since the first
day we met at Frascati ? All that time at Capri
was I not thinking of her, although persuading
myself that I was not interested in her personally ? How much less, then, could I forget her
after these two happy evenings. Yet, if ever any
one had a presentiment of misfortune in adopting
some particular course of action, I have. It is
not possible, of course, to do otherwise than
accompany them across the Brenner, since I
offered them my escort ; but I need not go to
Meran ; we can meet at Botzen. If she is to be

banished from my memory, it would be folly to
put myself in the way of sweet associations; of
seeing her constantly ; of walking and riding with
her ; guiding her through all the lovely excursions
about Meran. Then, indeed, I could never help
yielding to the charm of having such a companion—a charm which I have never known
before ; for in those fatal days when I fancied
myself in love, I was only caught by a beautiful
casket. It was so beautiful that it dazzled me,
and kept me from looking beyond. ʼ I took it for
granted that the jewel contained in it must be
priceless, until one day the casket flew open, and
showed me that the supposed jewel was a false
one. Now it is just the contrary ; the casket
boasts of no great beauty or outward ornament,
but may not the jewel within be precious ? Yes,
I see it is the lighting up of that jewel which
possesses so subtle a charm now, when no outward brilliancy could win a glance from me.
Were I sure of its intrinsic value, it would be
well worth the trial ; yet all kinds of dark fore-
bodings seem to warn me back. But how that
jewel's sparkle would brighten my cold, lonely
existence ! Shall I, then, go to Meran, or not ?"

Ah ! Flora, you little know how important a
moment this is for you ! Why are you not in
Venice, so that your presence might turn the

scale in your own favour ?　Will the memory
of yesternight's walk suffice for it ?　It appears
that at least it is sufficient to prevent sentence
from being pronounced against you.　The judge
is evidently not sure of himself; not sure that he
would have strength to carry it out, and therefore
he wisely defers putting it on record.　He will
wait and see what time will do.　So you may congratulate yourself on a half triumph, at all
events ; and occupy yourself with the sights of
Verona and the different beauties of the route to
Meran.

In "fair Verona's" amphitheatre, unmatched
save by the giant Coliseum of Rome, we left the
Adairs standing, and when they had wandered
up and down its tiers and given their meed of
admiration, they drove to see the house of the
Capulets and the—so-called—tomb of Romeo and
Juliet.　On their way Flora told Marie the lovers'
sad history, and showed her how doubly interesting
the site is to natives of Great Britain, because
enshrined in their great poet's genius.

An afternoon they found sufficient to "do" the
lions of Verona, so the next morning they started
by train for Peschiera, and there took the steamer
to Riva.

What a lovely sail it is across the Lago di
Garda, with its boundary of castle-capp'd mountains

and the little villages at their base, half buried in
groves of lemon and orange tress! And, for lovers
of classic memory, there are the ruins of the
house where Catullus dictated his ballads. In
the days of Virgil the lake was celebrated for
looking like a little sea, foaming beneath the lash
of the mountain winds, which seldom left it unruffled; and to-day it did not belie its reputa-
tion, as its blue waters tossed about in miniature
fury, the white-crested waves rolling one over
the other and dashing their spray afar. Riva
itself is a charming little place; and then the
drive to Trent—a drive which shows one of
Tyrol's greatest charms, that of uniting something of the wildness and grandeur of Switzerland
with the soft, fresh beauty of our home scenery.
. . . Now we see an isolated lake, so shut in
by snowy mountains that the only egress from its
shores seems to be a winding, giddy mountain
path, to which we almost fear to trust ourselves ;
but if we venture and ascend it for a time, we
find that it leads down, on the other side, into a
smiling valley, with emerald green fields stretching
far away in gentle undulations, and watered by
little rivulets flowing between flowery banks and
shady trees. Or we come suddenly upon two
rocky points spanned by a single plank, and at
such a height that, looking at it from below, it

appears as if it were suspended in the air; and beneath, a rushing torrent dashes over its rugged bed, gurgling and foaming at each attempted interruption to its headlong course. Let us climb down from this wild spot, and we come upon an almost English scene of comfort and neatness; there is a pretty cottage with its shelving wooden roof and carved cross in front; the sheep and cows are grazing at a distance, and the shepherd boy is lying in the grass pulling the wild flowers which grow around him. The character of Tyrol's inhabitants partakes too of all this; they have the open independent bearing of mountaineers, combined with rare simplicity and softness. There is not a spot in all Tyrol without its own beauty, and we should travel far indeed before we met so fine a race of people; not only in their general character, but also in their outward appearance.

The Adairs slept that night at Trent, and before leaving the next day they visited its churches, particularly the one where the great Council was held, and there they saw a painting of it which contains portraits of several of the prelates who assisted thereat. Towards evening they arrived at Botzen, just as the last rays of the sun were lighting up the Calvarienberg, as the mountain close to the entrance of the town is called, on account of the stations of the Cross which lead up

to the Calvary on its summit. With one accord
they all exclaimed, "How beautiful!" But in
Tyrol this is an exclamation which is called forth
at every turn, and words are indeed too weak to
express the different degrees of its loveliness.

How glad Flora felt at the prospect of getting
to Meran to-morrow! It would be the fourth day
since they had left Venice, the day upon which
Mr. Earnscliffe had promised to meet them; and
she looked forward anxiously to that meeting.
Once before she had parted from him in the utmost
friendliness, and when next she saw him he
scarcely spoke to her—would it be so now? These
were her thoughts as they drove along the hill
and castle-bordered route which leads from Botzen to Meran.

No familiar face greeted them at the Post Hotel.
The day waned, and Flora stood leaning listlessly
against one of the front windows, gazing down
the road which they had traversed that morning,
and sadly she thought: "So he is not coming—I
suppose he will wait until the exact time when he
thinks we shall want to cross the Brenner; but, at
least, he might have written to say so. It is rude
of him thus to break the appointment without a
word of apology. How slowly the days will now
pass, even here in beautiful Meran! Beauty and
pleasure are only accessories; they cannot give a

particle of the happiness which we may feel, even
in toil and trouble, when endured for one whom
we love. Moore was right when he said—

> ' Life is a waste of wearisome hours,
> Which seldom the rose of enjoyment adorns.' "

But stay: Flora's listless attitude changes;
she bends eagerly forward over the window sill,
then draws back and throws herself into an arm-
chair beside it. Her colour is bright and her eyes
are dancing. Whence this sudden change? We
have only to look along the Botzen road, and an
approaching carriage with a single occupant will
tell us the cause of it.

Flora Adair's eyes had not deceived her. Its
occupant was Mr. Earnscliffe. We remember, that
day when the Adairs left Venice, how he hesitated
about joining them at Meran; yet here he comes,
although it would be difficult to say what had turned
the balance in Flora's favour. They started on
Tuesday, and that day and the next Mr. Earnscliffe
spent in visiting different galleries with dogged
perseverance, although they did not seem to afford
him any great pleasure. He also went to see
some Italian artists and literary men with whom
he was acquainted, and for the remainder of the
time he made a feint of reading, whilst in reality he
was pondering on the Meran question. Thursday

came, and he half determined to be wise and stay
away. If he were to do so, however, he felt that
he must write to Mrs. Adair and say that he could
not leave Venice for some days, but would meet
them at Botzen a week hence, and have everything arranged for crossing the pass at once, if
he did not send an apology, he must of course
fulfil his promise to join them at Meran; however, it would be time enough to write in the
afternoon. He dawdled away the morning over
some books which had been lent to him, and then
prepared to go out; but just as he was about to
do so, in came an Italian who asked him to make
one of a party of five or six, himself included, who
were going by the next train to Treviso to see the
paintings of Titian and Domenichino, in the fine
but yet unfinished cathedral, and also the Villa
Manfrino; they would dine at Treviso and return
to Venice in the evening.

The Italian named those who were to be of the
party. Mr. Earnscliffe knew them all to be more
or less well-informed, agreeable men, and among
them were two excellent musicians and impro-
visatori; so at least the proposal held out to him
the prospect of hearing some good singing, of
which he was particularly fond; besides, it would
spend the day for him, and if he were candid
with himself he would acknowledge that he felt

rather at a loss for something to do. Accordingly he accepted the invitation and went off with his friend, without ever thinking of the note to Mrs. Adair.

The day passed quickly away, and the dinner was excellent; the champagne abundant; the singing of the best; the conversation flowing and animated—Mr. Earnscliffe sustaining a prominent part in it. He spoke Italian with perfect ease, and entering into the spirit of the hour, he showed how brilliant, without being shallow, were his powers of conversation, when he once cast off his habitual reserve. They only returned to Venice by the last train, which arrived about eleven, and Mr. Earnscliffe, having wished his friends good-night and thanked them for the pleasant day which they had afforded him, got into a gondola and soon landed at his hotel, the "Victoria."

The night was as lovely as the one upon which he had parted from Flora Adair. The memory of that night now rose up vividly before him, and as it did so, he remembered with pleasure that he had *not* written to Mrs. Adair, and that now it was too late to hesitate any longer; go he must. If he started by the first train in the morning, he could reach Meran the same evening, and so keep his appointment, and this he determined to do;

so as soon as he got into his room he rang for his
servant, and told him that he was to have everything ready for them to leave Venice by the
six a.m. train next morning. The servant looked
rather dismayed at this intelligence, but retired
without making any remonstrance; for he knew
that his master must be obeyed to the letter, and
unhesitatingly too.

As the door closed Mr. Earnscliffe exclaimed,
" So for good or evil it is decided that I go to
Meran. Perhaps it is as well that it should be so.
I shall have an opportunity of knowing Flora
Adair thoroughly. If she is all that I have
dreamed of, and if I can win her love, it will be
worth having suffered, even as I have done, in
order to taste such unexpected bliss; and if she is
not, it will be only one pang more, and what
signifies that in such a life as mine? Not to go
would be to throw away a chance of possible
happiness through fear of possible pain; and that
at best would be more of cowardice than pru-
dence. I am glad that I am going in spite of all
my presentiments."

On the following day Mr. Earnscliffe reached
Botzen about four. He dined there, and set out
afterwards in an open carriage for Meran, where
we have seen him drive up to the hotel. He left
his servant at Botzen to make inquiries about the

carriage and ascertain where was the best place for getting really good horses, and then he was to follow him to Meran.

Mrs. Adair and Marie met Mr. Earnscliffe just as he got out of the carriage. They were returning from the Friday evening devotions in the church, at which they had been present. Flora did not accompany them, for she felt that even if she did go she would be only corporally in the church, that her mind and heart would be fixed on the Botzen road and not on prayer; so she remained at home watching the setting sun, and with it fell her hopes of that longed-for arrival.

The sun sank, but her hope rose and broke into bright certainty.

Marie ran into her room, crying, "Flore, *Monsieur Earnscliffe est arrivé!*"

The waning light and the shadow which the curtain threw over Flora prevented the blush and conscious smile from being seen, as she answered, "Indeed, then he has been punctual to his word, I see."

"And we take tea downstairs with him, Flore, Madame Adair has told me to tell you. Are you ready?"

"I shall be before you, Mignonne, for I have only to brush my hair and wash my hands, and you have, besides all this, to take off your out-of-door

things ; but surely there is not any hurry if we are
to wait for Mr. Earnscliffe,—he must have time
to shake off the dust of the journey before •he
appears for the evening."

CHAPTER XVIII.

A WEEK is quickly passed in Meran in visiting the different places of interest in its neighbourhood—all so rich in the beauties of nature, yet richer still in the memories of the late war of independence in 1809, when Tyrol's children, headed by her peasant-hero, Andreas Hofer, rose in defence of their religion and their liberty, and with rare heroism maintained the struggle almost single-handed for several months—Austria having withdrawn her troops from Tyrol in the August of 1809—against the united and disciplined forces of France and Bavaria.

Close to the town are the hill and castle of Zeno, both so called because St. Zeno was consecrated in the chapel which, with the exception of one of the entrance towers, is the only part of the castle still standing. Looking from its summit over the broad range of the Janfen mountains—whose passes were defended like so many Thermopylæs—and the valleys which gave birth to those brave defenders, we cannot help recalling the following beautiful words of a German writer : " A wild river rushes by the castle-topped hill of Zeno, and in vain do the red roses bend lovingly over it, as if to soothe its foaming waters with their kisses ; in vain do the fig-trees spread over it the soft shade of their fresh green leaves ; unheedingly it dashes on with a deep sullen roar. What sort of a river is it then ? How comes it that the lovely flowers and the soft balmy shade cannot win it to anything like peace and rest? Ah ! that river is the Passer ! Does it then entone an eternal lament over the heroes whose lullabies it once sung, or is it that with unbridled fury it dashes on to the Etsch, so that, in union with it, it may look upon the land where the Sandwirth of Passeier laid down his heroic life."

A little more distant from Meran is the Schloss Tirol, the ancient residence of the country's princes, and from which it takes its name. There, too, it was that Hofer and Hormayer— Tyrol's simple mountain son, and proud Austria's baron—met on terms of equality to consult over the means to be taken in order to preserve the country's newly-won freedom. Then the castle of Schönna, magnificently situated at the entrance of the Passeier valley, now in possession of Archduke John's son, the Count of Meran, and many others scarcely less remarkable. But exceeding all other spots in interest is the Sandwirthshof, the birthplace and home of Andreas Hofer, the pure noble-hearted patriot whom Napoleon—to his everlasting shame—condemned to death and caused to be shot in Mantua on the 20th of February, 1810.

Thus from Meran our friends made excursion after excursion, and Mr. Earnscliffe almost ceased to struggle with his daily increasing admiration for Flora Adair; yet he rarely betrayed it by word or look, even whilst wandering by her side through scenes where almost every hill and castle made her eyes light up with enthusiasm, as she talked of the deeds connected with them. He delighted in exciting her about her favourite Tyrolese, and as they stood one evening a little in advance of Mrs. Adair and Marie, leaning over the rocky bridge which runs into the lovely valley of Kinele, with the sun's golden rays illuminating its narrow defile, he began to tease her about them, and spoke somewhat disparagingly of the Passeier peasants in particular, as a stupid, stolid race—with the exception of Andreas Hofer, of course. She looked up at him exclaiming—

"Oh, Mr. Earnscliffe, you cannot mean what you say! The people who combine unsurpassed bravery with the softest compassion of a woman's

heart cannot be called 'stolid.' Was there ever
a war so remarkable for deeds of heroic humanity
as this peasants' war? You know, of course, the
grand act of the Passeier, Sebastian Prünster,
when he was one of the outpost watchers on the
hill above Volders—how, when he struck with the
butt end of his gun the Bavarian soldier who had
crept close up to him through the underwood in
order to shoot him, he felt horror-stricken as he
saw him rolling towards the precipice, and at the
risk of his own life dashed after him, caught him
up in his arms, and carried him to the soft grass
above, and having staunched his wound and
given him bread and brandy to restore his
strength, cried, 'Ass that thou art! what brings
thee up here? Flee as far as thou canst from
me. It pains my inmost heart to think that I
should be obliged to kill thee thus without any
good cause.' . . . How those who loved Sebastian
Prünster must have gloried in him!"

Flora had never seemed so charming to Mr.
Earnscliffe as now. She ceased speaking and stood
with her slight figure drawn up triumphantly, and
one little hand resting on the ridge beside her. He
looked at her for a moment in silent admiration,
and then, bending low over her hand — low
enough for his lips to have touched it, but they
did not—he murmured, more to himself than to

her, "What would not any living man give to hear himself so spoken of by you!"

The sound of these words fell faintly on Flora's ear, and she scarcely dared to believe that she heard aright ; nevertheless she blushed as she turned away, saying, "They are waiting for us."

This was their last evening in Meran ; the next day they commenced the crossing of the Brenner to Innsbruck. If Flora's enthusiasm for her favourite Andreas Hofer and his brave followers had been excited by visiting the peaceful haunts of their early days in the dark Passeier valley, what must it be now when passing over the very sites of some of their most wonderful victories ! And after spending some days in Innsbruck, the focus and hotbed—the Marathon of Tyrol, as it has been called—of that glorious war, they set out for Munich by the Achen and Tegernsee route. Two hours of train travelling took them to Jenbach, and thence an open carriage was to convey them to Achensee, their journey's end for that day.

About three o'clock they drove up to the pretty rustic little inn called Scholastica, which stands at the top of the lake ; and after an hour or two spent in resting and dining they went out to explore the beauties of Achensee, and as the best way to do so they were told to row up to the other end of the lake and walk back along its shore. As

they rowed slowly, and stopped every now and
then to feast their eyes on its loveliness, it was
tolerably late by the time they got out of the
boat. Mrs. Adair and Marie walked on at once
along the path which leads back to the hotel ; but
Mr. Earnscliffe and Flora stood gazing silently on
the scene before them.

What pen could give a true idea of Achensee
at any time? . . . It would indeed be rash to
attempt to describe it on such an evening as this,
when it lay bathed in a flood of mellow light shed
from the golden slanting rays of the setting sun.
What words could paint that lake, so closely shut
in by mountains as to be almost hidden within their
bosom—their peaks towering one above another
with their still snow-covered summits glowing
with the rich red tints of the dying day; the
lengthening shadows creeping over its deep blue
waters, and gathering round Flora Adair and the
object of her love, as they stood on its brink?

Well do we know the indescribable beauty of
Achensee on a fine evening at sunset, for we too
have stood on its brink at that hour, gazing into
its waters, and watching the shadows flitting over
them, but

" Alone the while,"

that is, with the heart's void unfilled save by a

vague ideal. What must it be to stand there beside the one all-absorbing love of one's life! And
Flora knew what that was now, as she leaned
against a tree with her hat in her hand, the light
breeze ruffling her luxuriant hair.

"Miss Adair," exclaimed Mr. Earnscliffe, suddenly, "can you not picture to yourself in such a
scene as this the interview between Rudens and
Bertha in Schiller's 'William Tell'? . . . Oh! I
can feel with Rudens as he says,

> "Könnt ihr mit mir euch in das stille Thal
> Entschliessen und der Erde Glanz entsagen—
> O, dann ist meines Strebens Ziel gefunden;
> Dann mag der Storm der wildbewegten Welt
> Ans sichre Ufer dieser Berge schlagen—
> Kein flüchtiges Verlangen hab' ich mehr
> Hinaus zu senden in des Lebens Weiten—
> Dann mögen diese Felsen um uns her
> Die undurchdringlich feste Mauer breiten,
> Und dies verschlossne sel'ge Thal allein
> Zum Himmel offen und gelichtet seyn!"*

Flora, as if in a sort of dream, began Bertha's
answer—

> "Jetzt bist du ganz———"

---

* Canst thou then dwell with me in this peaceful vale, and
forego earth's pomp? Oh, then the goal for which I struggled is
attained, and the storms of the wildly agitated world may beat
unheeded against the firm bulwarks of these mountains. Not
one more fleeting wish have I to send forth through life's whole
expanse. Oh, now may these rocks around us here spread into
impenetrable encircling walls, and this blessed valley be alone
open to and lighted by heaven.

Bertha—Now art thou all———

She stopped suddenly, and got very red.

"Why do you stop, Miss Adair?" asked Mr. Earnscliffe, eagerly. "Why break the charm which you shed around me—that of being with one who responds to each implied thought and feeling?"

"I see that we have been carried away by Schiller's beautiful poetry even to the forgetting that mamma and Marie have preceded us by some minutes towards home. Pray let us make haste to overtake them," answered Flora, blushing more than ever, and moving away. Mr. Earnscliffe was at her side in a moment, and said, "Yes, we will follow them, but as we go you must hear me, Miss Adair. I can wait no longer to have my fate decided. Over each hill and through each dale of this lovely land have I wandered before, but never until now have I *felt* its beauty to the full; never until now have I known—to use your own poet's words—the 'soft magic' of having one, the beloved of my heart near me,

'To make every dear scene of enchantment more dear,'

Flora, will you hear me?"

She made a slight motion of assent, but did not look up, and he continued, "Yet I must not ask you for an answer until I have given you—

though painful be the task—a short sketch of my
life, so that you may know me as I *really* am before you decide for or against me, and also that hereafter none may have the power to tell you aught
of my earlier days that you have not already
heard from my own lips. . . . Left an orphan,
whilst still almost a baby, I was consigned to the
guardianship of an uncle, and most honourably
did he fulfil the trust; but I could no more love
that imperturbable, just man, who was *coldly*
kind upon principle, than fire and water could
blend. He was not married, so I had no aunt
or cousins to whom I could attach myself, and
it was a joy rather than a grief to me that I was
sent to school when very young. I applied with
unusual ardour to study, and gloried in the
power which I possessed of being first among
my companions, and in my facility for mas-
tering foreign tongues. . . . I lived among
the ancients—those master spirits of old who by
their nobility of soul rose above the debasing vice
of their age, and stood forth as bright examples
of the great power of man's own mind and will
unaided and unrestrained by the fetters of modern
society or Christianity. Thus I passed from a
studious, dreamy youth, to man's estate. I was
ardent and enthusiastic, full of glowing ideals of
moral beauty and excellence, and, with all the

prestige of high birth and wealth to assure me a favourable reception from the world, I was launched into the vortex of London life. I tasted of all its pleasures ; I was courted and sought after ; yet by most people I was looked upon as being

'Among them, but not of them ; in a shroud
Of thoughts which were not their thoughts.'

But what cared they for that? I was rich and successful, and was, therefore, to be flattered. At Lady M——'s ball—" . . . he paused, covered his eyes with his hand as if to shut out the stinging memories which now thronged before them; he mastered himself and went on, . . . "Pardon me, even now I cannot recall that time without a shudder, and only dare to pass cursorily over its events. . . . Well, as I said, at Lady M——'s ball I saw one who then appeared to me to be beautiful, and was introduced to her ; I was completely captivated. I imagined—ah, *now* I know, 'twas only imagination—that I loved her with a deep, true passion. I won her,—but scarcely had I time to congratulate myself on my conquest when I discovered—oh, that I should have to tell it!—that I had been deceived, betrayed by her; that she had accepted me only for my wealth and position, whilst her love was another's. To resolve to separate from her for ever was a moment's work, and I confided to the care of my lawyers all the necessary arrangements, and left England, to escape at least from the scene of my misery, and the rankling consciousness that men were laughing at the proud *exalté* Earnscliffe, who had been caught by the light beauty; then I awoke from the dream of careless enjoyment in which I had been living. . . . The face of nature in its calm repose seemed to mock at my wretchedness. Everything gave testimony of a creative power; but of justice, of love, in that dread power, I could see no trace. . . . I had not asked for life; I had done nothing knowingly to merit the curse which had fallen upon me. Why then was I subjected to a betrayal which blighted my every hope, dried up all the sources of happiness from which I used to drink?—for my belief in truth and goodness had been shattered. . . . I asked for what had I been created? Why doomed to bear unasked-for existence? . . . I sought eagerly for comfort in religion, but I could find none. What consolation could any man's interpretation of Scripture give me, since everything they said was vague and varying? I longed for some universal certainty—something upon which to lean with one's whole weight, but nowhere could I find it; the more I sought, the more incomprehensible did everything appear to me, seeing all around

as Lamartine says, 'evil where good might be.'—
At last with wearied brain and aching heart I
gave up the search. To end my life seemed to
me to be a cowardly thing; to plunge into dissi-
pation, as Byron did, beneath me; so I resolved
to be henceforth self-sufficing; noble and true,
because such qualities alone make man great; but
trusting in none, believing in nothing, and above
all, not in a woman. . . . Such has been my life for
the last ten years. But a few months ago there
came a break in its terrible monotony—I met you!
Accustomed as I was to be flattered and fawned
upon by young ladies as a good match, your
severe remark upon what I said to Mrs. Elton at
Frascati made me almost start with surprise, and
during the time when I considered myself bound
to visit you and try to relieve the wearisomeness
of your imprisonment, I studied you as something
new—unknown before. I became interested in
the study, nevertheless I would not admit to
myself the possibility that I could be attracted by
a woman. I persuaded myself that I merely felt
a curiosity about you; then I fancied that I had
discovered you to be just like the rest of your
sex, heartless and false, and, in spite of all my
theories about not caring for you, I mourned over
the supposed discovery. But a light was suddenly
thrown upon your conduct, and you came out

brighter than ever from under the cloud. . . . I
followed you on chance to Venice; I watched
you closely day after day in your family circle;
I saw how little the ordinary bagatelles and
vanities which sum up the existence of most
women occupied you, and I felt drawn towards
you as to a kindred spirit; yet I dreaded to trust
a woman again, and I struggled hard indeed
before I yielded to the charm of loving you. But
resistance was useless; the more I tried to think
of you as of others whom I had known, the more
I found you different, and at last I gave up the
struggle. Now I am yours wholly and entirely.
Refuse not then to receive the poor shipwrecked
traveller, who, having confessed to you all his
faults and misfortunes, clings to you as his last
anchor of hope on earth. . . . Flora do not hesitate
—speak." . . . He caught her hand and pressed
it tightly in his own.

The rush of wild delight, which thrilled through
every portion of Flora's being at having thus
offered to her a happiness so intense that she had
not dared to expect it, was so great, that for a
moment it deprived her of utterance; but raising
her glistening eyes to his, she gave him *such* a
smile that he asked for no words to interpret its
meaning, and drawing the already imprisoned
hand within his arm, he held it there clasped to
his heart, as he exclaimed—

" *My* Flora! this moment repays, nay, over-
pays me for all that I have suffered! . . . But
why do you tremble? Are you afraid of me?
Have you not faith in me?"

It cost Flora an effort to speak—to shake off
the exquisite emotion which the warm clasp of
his hand caused her to feel; but surely any lover
would have thought it an answer worth waiting
for when at length she said—

" You might as well ask me if I had not faith
in my own existence. All that I am afraid of is
the intensity of my happiness."

" Generous Flora! not one word of doubt,
although I could not offer you—what alone is
worthy of you—a heart's *first* homage; and yet
in very truth I might say that I never really
loved before. Now, indeed, can I forgive and
forget that faithless one——"

" And *I* can thank her for having left you free
to offer me the treasure of your heart, and to
receive mine in return whole and untouched—
friendship only has it known until now! But
'tis all that I have to give, for fortune I have
none, nor—as you see—beauty, and this last I
would that I had for your dear sake."

" But you have it for me, Flora. Your beauty
I would not have exchanged for that of a Venus
di Medici!"

"Nay, turn not flatterer, or I shall be forced to *begin* to doubt. But tell me, why did you treat me so icily when we met you at the Farnese Palace—to say nothing of the celebrated night at Mrs. Elton's?"

"So even then you noticed and felt my change of manner, Flora?" he asked in a low, thrilling tone, as he bent down and tried to get a full look at her face; but he could only see the bright red colour spreading even over her neck as she quickly turned away her head, and said gaily—

"Why, that is worthy of an Irishman! You answer my question with another, which I certainly shall not take any notice of; and now please to reply to mine."

"You shall be obeyed, my little queen. . . . The day before I met you at the Farnese Palace, Mary Elton told me that you were going to be married to Mr. Lyne, adding that, indeed, you could not *afford* to refuse such an offer as his. Prone as I was to believe that all women were ready to sell themselves, I scarcely doubted this to be true, although I knew that you did not particularly like Mr. Lyne. Then everything seemed to confirm it. I met you with him the next day at the Farnese Palace, and at Mrs. Elton's ball. He was constantly at your side. I saw you together

apart from everybody else, talking eagerly. At
last he stood up, and held your hand in his for
a moment before leaving you, and I believed this
to be the signing of the sale. I left Rome more
embittered than ever against women; but a chance
—a blessed chance—showed me how utterly
mistaken I had been. I learned from Helena
Elton that Mr. Lyne had proposed for you, but
that you—with a truth and courage rarely to be
found in woman—had refused him, rich as he
was, and although you yourself were portionless.
Oh, Flora! how my heart bounded to you from
that moment! Now you know all, and you see
that I not only love you ardently, but that I have
at the same time the highest esteem for you.
Come to me and be the chosen companion of my
heart and mind, for in you I pay homage to a
heart superior and a mind equal to my own!"

"It is worth. living for alone to hear such
words! But, again, I must chide you for flattery
and exaggeration, as it was both to say 'a mind
equal to my own.' No: mine is not equal to
yours—a woman's very education forbids it. Had
you said that I possessed a mind capable of understanding and following yours it might have
been true. Believe me, it is a woman's truest
glory to admit the great superiority over herself
of him whom she loves. What repose it is to trust

entirely in a higher being than one's-self,—to know
that henceforth you will be my lawgiver and
teacher; for you will have much to teach me
. . . But how sweet will such lessons be!"

"How could I have ever dreamed that I loved
before, oh, my dearest!"

"*I* can scarcely answer that question; but we
all know how tempting a bait is beauty of person
to you lords of the creation—is it not so? But
time wears, and I have much to say before we reach
the hotel. You have told me all your feelings
on religion. Another would shudder at such a
disclosure, and perhaps be scared from loving so
daring a spirit; but *I must* love you, whatever be
your faults. I believe I almost love your faults
themselves, because they prove what the strength
and grandeur of your character is; but I do shudder *for* you! How fearful it would be to think of
such a soul as yours lost for all eternity, and like
this glorious sun above us only shedding forth the
rays of its light and power for a few short hours
on earth, then setting into darkness, but unlike
the material sun, never to rise again. This must
not, shall not be if power or prayer of mine can
aught avail!"

Her face flushed and her eyes lit up with the
light of that long concentrated love which now
burst its bonds. To Mr. Earnscliffe it was irre-

sistible. He clasped her round the waist, drew
her to him, and—let Bulwer speak for us—"and
still and solitary deepened the mystic and lovely
night around them. How divine was that sense
and consciousness of solitude! How, as it
thrilled within them, they clung closer to each
other! Theirs was that blissful time, when the
touch of their hands clasped together was in itself
a happiness of emotion too deep for words!"

At length Flora said, as she walked on with
his arm still encircling her waist, "Yes, I do
hope that I may help you more than any theologian to reach the one great source of truth. Let
me say a few words of my own experience. . . .
Like you, when at school I delighted in study,
and enjoyed being first among my companions.
This, added to a cold although invariably polite
manner, caused me to be looked upon by the
rest as proud and haughty, setting myself apart
from them. But I was indifferent to others;
study and the approbation of one of my mistresses,
whom I dearly loved, were everything to me, and
as far as it went, I was perfectly happy within
those dear convent walls. My sorrow at leaving
them was great; but I could not spend my life
there. I too one day awoke from a dream of
careless, thoughtless happiness. That day came
when I left school to enter upon a young lady's

inane existence. I felt, as Schiller says, that 'empty
occupation cannot fill the soul's void; there is a
deeper happiness, there are other joys!' Balls,
visits, promenades and needle-work—what could
they give to satisfy the heart or the mind? The
people whom I met in society wearied me; I
longed for something different. Then I sought
for rest and contentment in religion, but I found
them not; and weary of the present and dreading
the future, I too asked, 'Can life be a gift?
Where am I to find the justice and goodness of
God of which I am told? Is it not He who has
made me *what* I am, and why, why render me
incapable of finding contentment in the ordinary
occupations of those with whom He chose to cast
my fate?' All the other stumbling-blocks to
human reason—predestination, the origin of evil
—followed in the train of these thoughts; I was
on the verge of losing all faith; but grace and
the teaching of one of God's own ministers, one
to whom I must ever owe the deepest gratitude,
saved me. He showed me the evidences and
truth of the Fall of man—that key to all knowledge
of him; he proved to me the existence of a Divine
teaching Authority, by which man could learn his
end, and the means of attaining it; he made me
see how absurd was the attempt of finite reason
to measure itself with the Infinite; and he summed

up all in these words, as he pointed to the crucifix, ' Will you refuse to believe in the goodness
of Him who gave his only Son to die on a Cross
for your sake? And, trusting to that goodness,
can you not wait patiently until the few short
years of life shall be over, and all shall be made
clear as noonday to you? On the other hand, if
you will not wait, if you refuse to submit your
reason, what will you gain? You say that you
are not happy now: will it make you happier not
to believe in eternal happiness, and throw away all
hope of attaining it? . . . How true was all this!
I could not doubt the life or divinity of our
Saviour: history itself proves it too clearly; then
how could I deny the great testimony of love
given in His Crucifixion? Again and again re-
curred to me that question: ' What will you gain
if you refuse to submit your reason?' Nothing,
absolutely nothing: nay, more, I began to see that
to dwell on these subjects, which are above, not
against, human reason, could only lead to misery
and perhaps to madness; and I determined to
question no more, but to believe. . . . ' Easier
said than done,' perhaps you will answer. . . .
True, it is easier said than done, but at least it
is possible in the only religion which bears the
impress of Divine foundation, the only religion
which dares to attribute to itself the delegated

authority of God, and say, 'So far and no farther shalt thou go.' . . . Study *that* religion, examine the proofs upon which its authority rests; but you must go to that study, that examination, with the full determination that as soon as you recognise its Divine foundation, you will trust to faith, and not to finite reason. I know it will ever be re-belling, but those rebellions must be crushed down with a firm hand. We cannot all be simple loving disciples like little Marie, but we can do our utmost, and say, 'My God, I am what Thou hast made me; accept then what I can give Thee.' "

She ceased speaking, and for a few moments they both remained silent; then Mr. Earnscliffe said gravely, "I *will* make the examination which you desire, with all earnestness and sincerity, and God only knows how I have longed for truth and certainty; but I could not venture to give you much hope that your wishes and my own will be crowned with success; nevertheless, you *have* done more towards making me a believer, my Flora, than any theologian, even though you admit that your mode of persuasion is second-hand; but you speak from your own feelings and experience, and not from theory, and with such an advocate how could I reason coldly?"

A look of love so inexpressibly tender rested on Flora, that her heart thrilled again with the intensity of her happiness. But at this moment they caught sight of a figure coming along the shady walk, now dimly lighted by the pale rays of the rising moon, and Flora gently disengaged herself from Mr. Earnscliffe's encircling arm. The approaching figure turned out to be Marie, who, as soon as she saw them, cried out, "Where are you gone? You have been so long time, Mrs. Adair is tired waiting you."

Flora could not think of any answer to give, but Mr. Earnscliffe said with mock gravity, "It is not at all wonderful, Mademoiselle, that we have been a long time coming, for we have had such a fall; and if I could only tell you what we fell into, you would not be astonished at our delay."

"Oh! vraiment," said little simple Marie, "I am so sorry; I hope Flore has not done herself harm. Relate me all that please."

"Never mind him, Mignonne; it is not true," said Flora, as well as she could speak from laughing.

Something, a nameless look about them both, suddenly struck her, and she exclaimed, "J'y suis maintenant, he means that—as you other English say—you have had a fall into love."

Flora, half indignant and half amused, said, "I declare you are too bad. I wonder what you will say next. But let us make haste to mamma; she must indeed be tired of waiting, and pray, Mignonne, do be *sage*. I assure you"—with a gay glance at Mr. Earnscliffe—"that our conversation has been awfully serious;—death, judgment, hell and heaven, are not more solemn subjects than those upon which we have conversed."

She took Marie's arm and hurried on, followed by Mr. Earnscliffe, who said, "This is not fair, Miss Adair; you surrendered yourself prisoner at discretion to me, and then on the first occasion you run away from me."

She laughed, but hurried on more than ever to the open space before the hotel, where Mrs. Adair was sitting admiring the silvery moonlit lake. "At last!" exclaimed Mrs. Adair as they came up; "I was almost getting frightened about you; and now let us go in and prepare for tea, which is no doubt ready."

Accordingly they went in, Flora managing that her mother and Marie should precede her, so that she might linger a moment to get one more fond clasp of Mr. Earnscliffe's hand and look of love. Then she too went in.

CHAPTER III

SHORTLY afterwards they came down to tea, Flora feeling very shy and conscious. When they had finished, Mr. Earnscliffe said he would go out to smoke a cigar; and as he left the room, he gave Flora a look which seemed to say that as soon as possible he would be glad to have some other company besides that of the cigar. Marie, with delicate tact, followed his example, declaring that she must go to her room to mend her dress, which she had torn. Then Flora went and knelt beside her mother and said, "Mamma, Mr. Earnscliffe has proposed to me."

"What! Mr. Earnscliffe—the woman-hater, as you used to call him!"

"He is not a *universal* woman-hater now, mamma," replied Flora, with a little smile of triumph.

"So it seems; but what answer have you given?"

"Mamma! can you ask?"

"Which means, I suppose, that you have

accepted him; but, my child, you know that
he is not a believer in religion. If he were to
become a Christian, then, indeed, I should not
object to him as a son-in-law; whilst he remains
in his present sentiments, however, you surely
will not think of marrying him."

Flora started up, saying, "Not think of marrying him! Oh! mamma! But he is virtually a
believer in Eternal Truth, if a yearning desire to
know it constitutes one; he could not be the man
he is, nor could I worship him so fully as I do, if
error had ever been capable of satisfying him.
From his early youth he has had a craving for
truth which has never yet been appeased; the
right means only have been wanting to lead him
into the body of the Church, and to give rest to
his soaring spirit. Then, mamma, do not, do not
in pity say that I must not marry him, or you
will break my heart; you will divide it between the
two whom I love best on earth. You know well that
no other man ever excited in me even a passing
fancy, and I love Mr. Earnscliffe as only a woman
can who has never loved before. I was _so_ happy
an hour ago when he asked me to be his, and now,
mamma, you will not turn my happiness into
wretchedness?" Flora knelt down again, and hid
her burning face in her mother's lap.

Mrs. Adair's eyes filled with tears as she wound

her arms round Flora, and said, "I cannot make you wretched, my precious one, when my only object on earth is your happiness; so I will not *forbid* you to marry him—besides, good seldom comes of *forbidding* marriages—but I beseech you to pause; take time to see if he will really become a Christian."

"*I* cannot oppose him, mamma; you may say anything you like to him about waiting, and if he consents to wait it is all right. I have no will but his, and I cannot begin to thwart him now when I ought to begin to practise that most sweet duty which is to be mine—the duty of obeying him even in trifles. Besides, his life has been so unhappy that it would be cruel in *me* to hesitate about granting whatever he wishes. Go to him, mamma, and do all you can to persuade him to wait for whatever time you wish to name, but do not ask me to join in opposing him—only let me be neutral."

"My poor child, I see yours is a hopeless case; but come with me, and I will say all that I think right before you."

Mrs. Adair kissed her again and again, then stood up, and putting her arm round her waist, led her out to meet Mr. Earnscliffe.

A little way down the walk they saw Mr. Earnscliffe leaning against a tree, and smoking

furiously; as soon as he perceived them, he
advanced quickly to meet them, and said, in an
eager tone, "You are come to give me Flora,
Mrs. Adair, are you not ? "

"I cannot keep her from you, Mr. Earnscliffe;
your conquest is indeed complete, so take her "—
and she placed Flora's hand in Mr. Earnscliffe's.
He kissed Flora's forehead warmly, then took
Mrs. Adair's hand, and put it to his lips as he
answered, "Oh, that I knew how to thank you,
Mrs. Adair! At least you shall see how I will
guard the precious trust which you now place in
my hands."

"Do not thank me, Mr. Earnscliffe; I give her
to you not as a free gift. Let us walk on,—I wish
to speak to you very seriously."

He turned, and drawing Flora's arm within his
own, he walked between her and Mrs. Adair,
murmuring in a low tone to Flora, "You are
mine now, indeed."

Mrs. Adair then began, "I said that I do not
give you Flora as a free gift, Mr. Earnscliffe, and
it is because you are not a believer in religion.
You possess everything else that I could possibly
desire for her in a husband, but what is there that
can make up for the want of faith? It is a fearful
risk for a Christian to marry an unbeliever; it
is endangering that faith without which ' it is

impossible to please God ; ' therefore I urged
Flora—as strongly as a parent could urge without
using authority—not to accept you. But, 'tis true,
one does not reason where one loves: she would
not listen to anything, and so implored me not to
make her wretched for life by refusing to let her
marry you,—that I could not do so. But I think
I have a right to ask that you should wait a year,
and try if you cannot during that time see the
truth of religion."

"A year! Mrs. Adair! If you knew what my
life has been, you would not ask me to wait so
long before I may enjoy the only gleam of sun-
shine which has been granted to me during ten
long lonely years. Give her to me at once, and
she will teach me better than any one else can. I
hope you do not think so badly of me as to
imagine that I would care less to arrive at the
knowledge of truth because I had already won
her. If you could feel what it would be to one
who has been buffeted about as I have been from
opinion to opinion, to find rest in certain truth,
you would not dread my leaving any means
untried in order to obtain it ; and to keep Flora
from me can make no difference, as even for her
dear sake I could not profess to believe unless I
did so fully. However, it shall be as Flora wishes.
I will abide by her decision whatever it may cost

me ; I would serve fourteen years for her, as we
are told that Jacob did for Rachel. Now, Flora,
say, must I suffer on through another year of
loneliness and misery? or will you trust me with
yourself at once, and have sufficient confidence in
me to believe that I will use every effort to do
and be all that I can to make you happy here and
hereafter?" He let go her hand as if to leave
her perfectly free, but she pressed her face against
his arm, as Mrs. Adair said earnestly, " Flora,
think what it is for a Christian to marry an
unbeliever! Let there be this year's trial, and
such a sacrifice to the advice of the Church will
merit happiness for you both."

"Yes," added Mr. Earnscliffe, bitterly, " and
so needlessly inflict twelve long months of suffering on him whom you love, and who for ten
years has known nothing else—this, too, merely
in obedience to the advice of your Church. If *it*
gives you leave to marry me at once, will *you*
refuse me? Flora, is it to be so?"

Poor Flora! what would she not have given
not to be called upon to decide the question, to
grant Mr. Earnscliffe's prayer. She knew that it
was an act of weakness to consent to his wishes,
but she had not the almost superhuman courage
to inflict such pain as her refusal would give him,

and from her own lips, too! No, she could not
do it, and with her head still pressed against his
arm, she murmured, "Mamma, I told you that I
could not oppose Mr. Earnscliffe in anything
which was not in *contradiction* to our Holy Faith.
If he chooses me to marry him at once I must do
it—that is, if I am permitted, and you do not
positively forbid me."

"My own true Flora!" exclaimed Mr. Earnscliffe.

"God help her, poor child!" said Mrs. Adair,
with a sigh.

"Do not say God help, but God bless her,
Mrs. Adair. Had I your faith I would say God
bless her ten thousand times over for her perfect
trust in the world-wearied man."

Flora glided away from Mr. Earnscliffe's side,
and went round to her mother, to whom she
clung fondly, saying, "But you must not be
angry with me, mamma; I could not help it; and
you must bless me too, or it will be a miserable
closing to a happy day. You must not make me
feel that my love for him is pain to you—it
would be too dreadful if *the* two strong feelings
of my life were to clash."

"They shall not clash, my darling child, and
of course I will bless you. I only want you to be

happy; but I fear that you are grasping *too* eagerly at happiness—what if it were to be taken from you?"

Flora shuddered from head to foot, and cried, "Oh, don't, don't, mamma dearest,—let me be happy whilst I may without thinking of dark possibilities; only bless me and"—in a low tone—"him!"

Mrs. Adair kissed her with overweaning affection, and said, "God bless you, my own sweet child, and give him whom you love the great boon of Faith.   Take her again, Mr. Earnscliffe, she is indeed yours."   Once more she placed her hand in Mr. Earnscliffe's, who again drew her round to his side as he replied—

"Mrs. Adair, I can only say, as before, that you shall see how little cause you will have to regret letting me have her at once.   And let it be all arranged now.   When may we be married?"

"We expect to reach Paris in about ten days; there, if you choose; all the necessary preparations can be made, and the marriage solemnized."

"That will answer so nicely.   From Paris I can take a run to England, and have the settlements—of which you and I, Mrs. Adair, can speak at our leisure—drawn up."

"There are not any settlements to be made, Edwin," said Flora, shyly, and for the first time

calling him by his Christian name; "you know
I have not any fortune."

"But I must make a provision for all future
possibilities. Suppose, for instance, that you were
to be left a widow; you must have a jointure."

"You are as bad as mamma, I declare—you
both seem to foresee nothing but misfortunes for
me."

"Heaven forbid!" exclaimed Mrs. Adair. "But
we had better go in now; it is getting late and
chilly."

"Chilly, mamma! why I find it quite hot, and
it is so beautiful out here; really one does not
know which to admire more, Achensee by sunset
or by moonlight—it is exquisite at both times."

"I daresay *you* find it so," replied Mrs. Adair;
"but I can answer for it its beauty does not keep
me warm. Besides we ought to go in to Marie—
she will feel so alone."

"That's true—how selfish I was to forget poor
little Mignonne! she *will* feel alone."

They walked back to the hotel, and Mrs. Adair
went in; Mr. Earnscliffe and Flora remained out
a few minutes more. He thought he had a right
to get a parting embrace from his betrothed, and
Flora was not prude enough or coquette enough
to try to withhold it from him. She could no
more think of being capricious or tantalising

towards her lover than she could of treating him coldly in order to increase his fervour,—as she had said to her mother, her only thought was how best to please him. The playfully capricious school of heroine is, we know, the favourite style in novels, but is not Shakespeare's Juliet a higher conception of a loving woman, as she says—

> " But trust me, gentleman, I'll prove more true
> Than those that have more cunning to be strange?"

Mrs. Adair's voice was heard calling, "Come, Flora." Mr. Earnscliffe let her go, saying, "I believe, after all, I must learn quickly to love God, that in perfect faith I may be able to ask Him to bless thee."

They joined Mrs. Adair, who said, holding out her hand to Mr. Earnscliffe, "Good-night. It is already late, and we start early to-morrow, so we must rest now."

"So soon, Mrs. Adair? But you have granted me so great a boon to-night that I cannot object to anything you wish; you have made me your most grateful and obedient subject for ever. Good-night then," and he kissed her hand.

They looked round for Flora, but she had disappeared. Mrs. Adair smiled, and said, "I dare say you have wished her good-night already, and she probably did not want to have the

private good-night spoiled by a public one, so ran
away."

Mr. Earnscliffe smiled too, as he handed Mrs.
Adair her candle, and taking his hat he went out
again.

Mrs. Adair was right. Flora had run away—
she had gone up to Marie. As she entered the
room the light of the moon showed her Marie
sitting in the window, looking sadly dejected, and
going over to her she put her arms round her,
saying, " Poor darling Mignonne !"

Large tears rolled slowly down Marie's cheeks
as she said in French, " Don't think me ill-
natured, Flore—don't imagine that I would not
do anything that I could to promote your happiness, but I felt so lonely ; I felt that I was a
stranger amongst you. Now that you are with
me, however, and as fond as ever, it is all well,
and I am so glad if you are happy, Flore. But
Monsieur Earnscliffe is not *un croyant,* so I suppose
you cannot marry him until he becomes one ?"

Flora felt almost angry with Marie. Was there
never to be an end of this question of religion ?
She subdued the feeling, however, and answered
gently, " Mignonne, if Mr. Barkley were not a
croyant, as you say, and if he came to you and
told you how for years and years he had known
only suffering, but that now he loved you and

that you could make him forget it all if you
would marry him at once, would you—could you
say to him, ' No, suffer on until you become one
of the body of the faithful ?' Could you condemn
him you love to endure pain which *you* could
relieve ? Could you refuse, even for a time, to
fulfil the office for which woman was created—
that of consoling and rendering happy one whom
she loves ?"

" I know it would be fearfully difficult," replied
Marie, looking very much puzzled ; " but if you
were told it was right to do so, what then ? "

" If the Church *forbade* me to marry him I
would of course submit. But what misery it would
be to make him endure one hour's suffering from
which I might save him. Thank God, I know
that there is no *indispensable* obstacle to my
marrying him—it would be *too* dreadful."

" Take care, Flore, there may be some *indispensable* obstacle although you know it not."

" Mignonne, wish me joy at having won the
love of *such* a man, rather than suggest obstacles
to our happiness ; it is a bad omen to hear of
nothing but objections on the night of one's
betrothal. God knows that ' sufficient unto the day
is the evil thereof,' " and again Flora shuddered.

" I do wish you joy, Flora, now and for ever,
and I will daily pray that Monsieur Earnscliffe

may soon be as firm a believer as you are yourself."

" Thanks, dear Mignonne, it is so unselfish of
you to think about me now in the midst of your
own trial."

" I was not unselfish a few minutes ago, Flore,
when I saw you and Monsieur Earnscliffe together, and his kiss of betrothal imprinted on
your brow made me cry ; yet indeed it was not
that I envied you, Flore, but it made me feel how
different everything was for me."

" You need not tell me that it was not envy,
Mignonne. I verily believe that you would not
know envy if you were to see it, so you might
indeed answer with regard to it as Nelson did
when somebody spoke to him of fear, 'What's
fear ? I never saw it.' "

" It is very *gentil* of you to say so, Flore; but I
want to talk about yourself. I want you to tell
me all about it,—how long you have cared for
Monsieur Earnscliffe ; when you discovered that
he liked you,—everything, *enfin*."

" It will only pain you, Mignonne,—only recall
Florence."

" But it will be such sweet pain, Flore ; do
tell me ?"

" Yes, anything you like, darling," answered
Flora, who certainly was just in the mood to-night

to do whatever could give anybody pleasure. So they had a long chat over this prolific subject to young ladies—a love affair. Then Flora went in to Mrs. Adair, and nearly an hour passed before she sought her own room.

It was the last on the corridor, and had a balcony looking upon the lake, so she was tempted to go out and look again on the beautiful scene without. To any one Achensee would have looked surpassingly lovely on that clear moonlight night, but to Flora Adair its beauty spoke with one of those voices "which set the inmost music of our souls a-going," singing a song which requires no words, yet breathing a prayer to heaven to be made more worthy of ministering to the object of our love, and to be enabled to make him happy. At length she muttered half aloud, " What bliss it was to hear him say that I had done him good! —my Edwin! "

" Flora ! "

She started, but more with pleasure than fear, at the sound of her own name, as she saw Mr. Earnscliffe come from under the shadow of the trees and stand facing the balcony as he said, " I saw you come out, and I have been watching you ever since. It was so delightful to see you there, and know that you were thinking of me. I even heard a sound which seemed very like Edwin;

but it would have been still more delightful if I
could have been standing up there beside you."

Flora blushed and laughed as she answered,
"Well, I must say it was very wicked of you to
be out here eaves-dropping when you ought to
have been in bed; and pray, why are you not
there?"

"Might I not ask the same question, fair lady?"

"No, it is quite a different thing for me. A
lady may have work and a thousand other things
to keep her up, but a man has no such excuse." .

"And does standing on a balcony in the moonlight get a lady's work done for her?"

"*Such* a question does not merit any answer.
But you will go in now, will you not? It is
really very late."

"Do you *wish* me to go?"

"I think you ought to go."

"That is not saying whether you *wish* me to
go or not; if you do, I will go."

"Unfortunately wish and ought are very often
at variance, and so they are now; wish says,
'stay out and enjoy this beautiful night,' and
ought, 'go in and to bed.' But now I must
obey *ought* for I have been very refractory of late."

"In what?"

"In not listening to its voice, which told me
to wait a year before I gave a certain person of

my acquaintance the right to plague me with his presence at all seasons and hours; so now goodnight indeed."

"Stay a moment longer, Flora; do not go yet."

" If I stay a moment it may probably stretch into an hour, and it really must not be ; good-bye again, but only till to-morrow." She retreated into her room as he kissed hands to her ; the window was closed, and he too went in for good.

We can imagine that, although it was very late when Flora got to bed, she was up betimes next morning, and took a stroll before breakfast, and of course it is unnecessary to say that her stroll was not a solitary one. Again they wandered down that walk which borders the lake, —that lake which evermore will be mirrored in Flora's memory as she saw it at eventide with the snowy mountains around it, crimsoned by the setting sun; then as it lay calm and unruffled in the pale silvery moonlight; and lastly as on that morning when the sun shone full upon it, and a light breeze tossed its waters into sparkling, dancing waves. It will ever be to her

> " The greenest spot on memory's waste."

When they got a little way from the hotel, Mr. Earnscliffe said, " Mrs. Adair was so kind as to say that all the arrangements for our marriage could be made in Paris, and that she expects to arrive there in about ten days, but I want *you* to name the day when you will give yourself to me 'for better, for worse.' I feel a feverish impatience to have you in my own keeping—to be certain that nothing on earth can separate us more."

"What could separate us now, Edwin?"—she pronounced his name shyly; then laughed and looked up at him, saying, "Do you know that I still feel half afraid to call you by your Christian name; it sounds so strange that *I* should have the right to take such a liberty with so grand and unapproachable a personage as you are."

"What, child, afraid of your captive! You ought rather to triumph in your victory over one who made so fierce a resistance; and pray don't have the least fear of wounding your captive's pride by taking *such* liberties with him. You can never know how sweet it sounded to him last night when first he heard you say Edwin."

"Well then, Edwin, I ask again what could separate us now? Surely you have ceased to doubt me, and know that the chains in which you hold me cannot be riveted any tighter; the marriage ceremony will only bless them, and give me its sacred sanction to dwell in the mighty shadow of your love."

"Ceased to doubt you, dearest! Of course I have. There is no real love without trust; but I want you to be mine beyond the reach of all danger. I am like a man who has found some rich treasure in an open field, and can feel no rest or peace until he can convey it into his house and revel in its possession; until then he dreads, he knows not what, but that something may rob him of what is so precious to him. But does the treasure not wish to be taken home? Would it rather be left where it is for some time longer?"

" Oh, Edwin!"

" Then, the day, Flora—the day!"

She paused for a moment, and then said in a low tone—

" The happiest day I have ever known until now was the 21st of June, the great feast of my dear school days, and its happiness consisted in the power of being nearly all the time with my favourite mistress, the object of my girlish love; so let my wedding day be the 21st of June, that day which will give me the unutterable happiness of being always with the love of my riper years; and thus the 21st of June will be to me the happiest day of my life in youth as in childhood. Are you satisfied, Edwin?"

She blushed all over as she spoke, and still

more so when his answer was to fold her in his arms, and murmur—

"My wife, then, in a few weeks hence!" Then he added, letting her go, but making her lean upon him again, "I will write to England immediately and desire all the papers to be got ready, so that I shall only have the signing work to do when I go there from Paris."

"But you will not be long away, Edwin, will you?"

"Trust me, I'll not stay longer than is absolutely necessary; but I must pay a flying visit to Earnscliffe Court to give orders about its being fitted up for your reception. Shall I take you to it—my real home—at once, darling?"

"Please, Edwin. Would it be possible to get there from Paris without stopping on the way? That would be so pleasant."

"So it would; and I'll think about how we can manage. The old place will bring up many painful memories, for I have not been there for more than ten years; but you will exorcise all those ghosts of the past, my Flora."

"It shall not be my fault if I do not, Edwin."

"Then in September I must whirl you off to Capri. I promised my poor fisherpeople there to go and see them again as soon as I could; but I almost doubt if they will know me, for I shall have grown so young-looking in this new atmosphere of happiness. How much I shall have to show you on those classic shores!"

"How bright a picture, Edwin: its brightness dazzles me. Oh, that it may be realised!"

"Why should it not be realised? *Now I* may ask, why do you doubt it?"

"Because it is too—too bright for me, Edwin. But we must return, or we shall be late for breakfast, and then mamma will not be pleased."

When they got into the breakfast-room, they found Mrs. Adair and Marie there. Flora had jestingly told the latter that she must congratulate Mr. Earnscliffe the first time she met him; but, of course, never meant that she should take it seriously. However, as Mr. Earnscliffe shook hands with Marie and wished her good-morning, she said, timidly—

"I wish you much happiness, Mr. Earnscliffe; and it would be very astonishing if you were not happy when you shall have Flore."

"I quite agree with you, Mademoiselle Mignonne: it *would* be very astonishing. But what do you say of Flora? If you were in her place, would you likewise say that it would be very astonishing if you were not to be happy?"

"Oh, that is all another thing, Monsieur. I would have fear of you; but Flora has not."

This speech of Marie's caused a general laugh, which covered the poor child with confusion; but Flora said gaily—

"Never mind, Mignonne! What you said was perfectly true :—I am not dreadfully afraid of the formidable Mr. Earnscliffe. I don't suppose that he will chop me up into mincemeat. But here comes the coffee, and we must not let it get cold."

CHAPTER IV.

ABOUT an hour after breakfast the carriage came
to the door, and our friends set out for Tegernsee,
two of them, at least, looking back fondly on
Achensee's secluded shores, and promising themselves to visit them again when their happiness
should be still more complete.   Promises, alas,
which might never be fulfilled!   Live in the
present, poor lovers—draw from the passing hour
all its sweetness ; but dream not of bliss to come !
The dark curtain which veils the future may too .
soon be drawn aside, and leave you standing face
to face with a stern reality.   Wander yet awhile
in lovely Tyrol!—feast your eyes on its green
valleys, where graze the peaceful flocks, and the
tinkling of their bells sounds musically through
the clear air, and look up to the mountain's height
where

> "Mortal foot hath ne'er or rarely been,"

or by the foaming torrent's course, and see there
the touching symbols of their faith, raised by

Tyrol's sons to cheer and guide the daring chamois hunter on his lonely way. It is a land that breathes of love and peace. Linger in it, then, and deem not that Paris, with its false glitter and turmoil, will crown your happiness. Passions fierce and angry dwell within that great city's walls and point their arrows towards you!

Immediately after leaving the village which lies at a little distance from the lake, the road to Tegernsee enters the narrow pass of Achen, bordered on one side by a rapid stream, and on the other by high mountains, which are so thickly wooded that even beneath a mid-day sun they make the pass look dark and solemn; whilst through breaks in the mountain's chain glimpses may be caught of smiling valleys, and here and there a solitary cottage.

In passing by a shrine the driver raised his hat, and Flora said in a low tone, " Do you condemn that, Edwin?"

" Not in these poor people, because they do not know that it is superstition."

" But suppose that it is *not* superstition, as you yourself will admit when you see the supernatural truth of religion, and God grant that that may be very soon."

"Amen! How I long for faith in *eternal* happiness now, Flora."

His expressive eyes and the tone of his voice
as it lingered over her name told all that words
did not say of why it was that he so longed for
such faith *now*. And Flora read it all therein
with deep delight as she answered, "How true
it is that the more the heart loves, the more
irresistibly is it drawn to Divine faith, for *then*
we dare not believe that the grave is to be the end
of everything. The great mystery of life and
death would be too awful had we not faith and
hope. So you must have them, Edwin."

"I shall have them, Flora, if I can only find
what I used to call my *ignis fatuus*—certainty—
to rest them upon. I gave up the search for it
long ago, as I told you, but now I will begin it
again in a new territory and under new auspices,
and if it will cease to be an *ignis fatuus*, and
blaze into a steady flame, how grateful I shall be,
and how I shall bless the star which lighted it up
for me, and shed over me the halo of happiness
for this world and for the next. But here we are
at the baths of Kreuth."

"It is very pretty," replied Flora, "although it
cannot boast of Achensee's grand wild beauty.
What could rival that?" Flora's smile seemed to
say that Achensee had more charms for her even
than those which nature had bestowed upon it.

At Kreuth a rest and hot luncheon—or dinner,

as it may be called—were very acceptable after
their drive through the keen mountain air; and in
about two hours they resumed their journey.
Some time before reaching Kreuth they crossed
the Tyrolian boundary into south Bavaria, where
the scenery all the way to Tegernsee is very
lovely, although, as Flora said, it cannot boast of
great wildness or grandeur; and Tegernsee itself
is a sweet little spot, but wholly devoid of any of
the characteristics of Achensee. The lake is like an
immense sheet of crystal, with pretty little villages
and gardens running down to its very edge, and
all around wooded hills and flowery meadows
meet one's gaze, but there is nothing solemn or
impressive about it. The dark blue lake shut in
by ramparts of snowy mountains, the isolated
cottages with their carved crosses, the oratory and
the shrine—these all belong to Tyrol. Tegernsee
charms the eye with its smiling prettiness and
brightness, but it does not speak to the imagination as Achensee does.

Our party stopped that evening and the next
day at Tegernsee, exploring its neighbourhood.
Walking was the order of the day. Mr. Earnscliffe
managed that they should drive as little as
possible; he declared that it was a shame not to
walk when there were such beautiful shady alleys
leading to all the different *points de vue* and

places of resort; or in other words, walking suited
his taste better than driving, because then he
could have Flora more to himself, whilst Mrs.
Adair and Marie preceded or followed them, as
the case might be.

Mr. Earnscliffe was an exacting lover, but he
could not be too much so for Flora; she asked
nothing better than to be with him, whether he
spoke or was silent, and he was very often silent.
On one occasion when they had walked for some
distance in silence, he said, " You are so good to
stay with me, Flora, in whatever mood I may be.
Does not my silence sometimes weary you? I fear
I seem but a sorry lover, and you never try to
make me what you would wish me to be ; you do
not use your privilege of *fiancée*—that of ruling
your lord elect."

" How can you ask if your silence wearies me,
Edwin ? Do you not know that silence is often
more eloquent than words ? It is enough for me
to be with you, and to feel that although you do
not speak, you like to have me at your side, and
would miss me were I to go away. And as to
ruling you, it would be no privilege to me,—I
want to be ruled. *Our* sovereignty consists in
voluntarily yielding to one whom we love, whilst
knowing that we have the power to give him happiness. This and this alone is our true sovereignty."

" Darling! what should I do if anything were
to take you from me ? " and he shivered.

Flora had observed that the fonder he appeared
to be of her the more did he seem haunted by a
morbid dread of losing her, and she asked,
" What makes you fear that anything should
take me from you ? "

" Because you are so precious to me, child, and
I am so unaccustomed to happiness that I can
scarcely believe in its realisation. I wish we were
married and that I had you safe at Earnscliffe
Court." He could not tell her about Mary Elton
and his strange dream;—of the former he was of
course bound in honour not to speak, and of the
latter it seemed so foolish and superstitious even
to think; yet it was the remembrance of these
which so often made him thoughtful and silent.

Flora saw that he was in a desponding mood,
and in order to distract him from his gloomy
thoughts, she began to question him about
Earnscliffe Court, what the grounds and house
were like, until by the time they reached the
term of their walk he was talking gaily about the
fitting up of the rooms for her reception, and as
the others joined them he appealed to Mrs. Adair
for advice on the subject.

In such walks and talks time slipped quickly
by—time, that tyrant which ever flees when we

would have it stay its course, and drags when we would give worlds to have it accelerate its speed! . . . How its wheels are going now for Mr. Earnscliffe and Flora! They are tearing up the hill at full speed, but at the summit the drag will be put on, and the descent will be slow and weary.

The morning but one after their arrival at Tegernsee they drove to Holzkirchen, and there got into the train for Munich. At the terminus Mr. Earnscliffe's servant, who had been sent on to engage rooms, met them with a carriage to take them to the Hotel des Quatre Saisons, where apartments had been taken for them.

How well does Munich merit its title of the Athens of Germany, with all its art repositories! Its fine wide streets and gay shops, too, claim for it a share of admiration from the lovers of hand-some modern cities. A week passes quickly there, and even then we come away without having really seen all its treasures, as it would indeed take a long time to exhaust the resources of its different galleries. In the old Pinacothek there are original paintings of the Spanish, Flemish, French, and Italian schools. Of the last-named school we see subjects from the pencil of its very earliest pupils,—Cimabue, Giotto, Sodoma, and Beato Angelico. And standing be-fore a picture of the *Frate's* we find Mr. Earnscliffe and Flora, the day after their arrival in Munich; Mrs. Adair and Marie had just gone into one of the other rooms.

" Do you like Fra Angelico's pictures ? " asked Flora.

" Yes, he is an exquisite painter."

" Yet he was, according to your ideas, an ignorant monk, and a worshipper of images; nevertheless, I daresay that your enlightened Landseer could not paint anything to equal his angels ! Yet he is generally considered to be one of your best painters."

" But it's not fair, Flora, to compare them," answered Mr. Earnscliffe, laughing at the mere idea of such a comparison ; " Fra Angelico's and Landseer's are altogether different styles."

" Of course they are. How could reason and truth, and superstition and ignorance produce the same style of painter ? And it was just that which struck me ;—the difference in elevation of style and subject shown by the disciple of truth and intellect over the poor superstitious monk ! "

Mr. Earnscliffe smiled, but remained silent, and Flora said, " Why do you not answer, Edwin ? Have I annoyed you ? "

"Annoyed me? No. I did not speak, because I was thinking over your words. It *is* strange, no doubt, that the painters of the Middle Ages should be of so much higher an order than those of our own time. To be candid with you, this reflection has often occurred to me before now, but I turned away from it as one of the many riddles which reason could not explain—I wish it could be satisfactorily cleared up."

"It *can* be, Edwin. But we shall lose mamma if we do not go on—she and Marie have already left this hall. . . . "

It would be too fatiguing to follow them in all their sight-seeing labours. The only expedition in which we feel inclined to accompany them is the one which they made to the Bavaria. Mr. Earnscliffe said that it was at a pleasant walking distance from the town; accordingly they went on foot, he leading the way with Flora. Both she and Marie were most curious to see the statue of a woman whose head alone can contain six persons, and they found it difficult to believe that it did not look like an overgrown monster. But, on the contrary, when they reached it they saw only the form of a beautiful woman standing on a marble pedestal and a lion crouching by her side. Its proportions are so admirable, that even when close to it they could hardly force themselves to credit its gigantic size.

The girls said they would like to ascend, just

for curiosity. Mr. Earnscliffe of course went with them. They sat down in the head, then looked through the eyes for a moment or two, but were glad enough to come down again, as the heat was excessive. When they returned and got again into the open air, they saw, much to their astonishment, a lady and gentleman speaking to Mrs. Adair, and heard her say, "How surprised they will be to see you here."

The lady turned round, and they saw Helena Elton, looking brighter and gayer than ever. Surprise was indeed depicted on all their countenances, but in Mr. Earnscliffe's there was another expression blended with it which was not so easily read.

"Helena Elton!" exclaimed Flora.

"Helena Elton is no more," she said, laughing and blushing; "allow me to present my husband, Mr. Caulfield."

When the excitement caused by this unexpected meeting had subsided a little, Mrs. Adair said, "Had we not better return now? We dine at five to-day, so as to be ready to go to the Opera, which begins at six."

"We are going to do so also," added Mr. Caulfield."

"Then, Helena, you might as well walk back

with us; I want to hear a great deal of news,"
said Flora, with a significant glance at Mr.
Caulfield.

" Indeed, Miss Flora, and do you expect me to
gratify your curiosity? But come, I will indulge
you if you will promise to gratify mine in return."

" If I had anything to tell which could gratify
it, I might promise, but one can't make promises
if there is nothing to be told; however, we can
make terms as we go," answered Flora, lightly.

" Very well, so be it. We drove here, but we
can send away the carriage, can't we, Harry?"

" To be sure we can, Cricket; I dare say the
driver will not be inconsolable for the loss of our
company if he gets our money. But, Mrs. Adair,
can you not wait for a few moments to let us run
up Dame Bavaria,—we want to be able to say that
we have been in a woman's head."

" Yes, ten minutes cannot make any great
difference."

" Oh, we shall do it in less time than
that."

As soon as they had got into the statue,
Mr. Earnscliffe drew Flora aside, and said, " Do
not tell her of our engagement. I will give you
my reasons for not wishing it to be told to her, at
another time."

" It is enough to know your wishes in order to

follow them, Edwin; you can tell me the reason
when you like, or not at all, if you choose. But
I must caution mamma and Marie."

He pressed her hand as she turned away from
him and went to her mother. Shortly afterwards,
Mr. and Mrs. Caulfield came down again, and
they all set out to walk home, Mr. Caulfield
having first discharged their carriage.

Helena and Flora walked together, as pre-
arranged, and the latter thought the best way
to keep from admitting her engagement was to
begin by telling as much as she chose, and so
prevent too much questioning; therefore, she said
at once, "When you talked of my gratifying
your curiosity, Helena, I suppose you meant to
allude to Mr. Earnscliffe's being with us, but, alas !
for your gratification, there is very little to tell.
We met him by chance in Venice."

"Chance, Flora?" interrupted Helena.

"Yes, quite so; we did not even know that he
was in Venice. We happened then to speak of
crossing the Tyrol. Mamma said we were going
in the diligence,—as we were three unprotected
females she did not like to take a carriage and
trust altogether to the driver of it,—when
Mr. Earnscliffe good-naturedly offered to escort
us over the pass. That is all I have to tell
you."

"Come, Flora, you are not so verdant as to imagine that a Grand Mogul like Mr. Earnscliffe, who, as a general rule, dislikes ladies, would offer to dance attendance upon three of them out of mere good nature; it is quite evident that he would never have done so unless one of the three had pinioned him with Cupid's fiery darts. Admit, Flora, that he is in love with you."

"Well, Helena, your reasoning *is* worthy of a woman, for it is utterly guiltless of all logic. Because a gentleman offers to see us across a mountain pass, you jump to the conclusion that he must be in love with *me*. If even it were—which, of course, it is not—a necessary consequence of his travelling with us that he should be in love with one of the party, why, in the name of all that's wonderful, fix upon me? Marie is much prettier. Why, then, not upon her?"

"Prettier—yes; but you might as well talk of his being in love with me as with her. Why, he considers *us* merely good, gay little fools, that is, if he could for a moment bring down his great mind to think about us at all. Of course, *you* are the 'favourite;' and if he does not propose it will be very dishonourable."

"How can you be so absurd, Helena?" said Flora, getting a little excited, yet feeling that too warm a defence might only betray her. "It

would be too bad if a gentleman could not do a
good-natured act to three ladies without being
expected to propose for one of them, and surely
an avowed woman-hater like Mr. Earnscliffe could
do it most safely without giving cause for any
such expectations. But never mind *him*,—I want
to hear about yourself. I need scarcely say that
I knew there was a flirtation between you and
Mr. Caulfield in Rome; but I had no idea that
Mrs. Elton would approve of him as a suitor for
your hand."

"Approve of him, indeed! What an idea!
Poor Harry is not enough of a big-wig or rich
enough to take my lady mother's fancy. Our
history is quite a romance."

"Then please to let me hear it, or a *résumé* of
it, at least, for we have not much time to
spare."

"Well, then, to begin at the beginning. Early
in the winter Harry and I became great friends,
and at first mamma seemed to be amused with
him, and used to laugh at our incessant skirmish·
ing. Then that day at Frascati—you remember
it, Flora?—she suddenly got up the idea that I
flirted *too* much with him. She was particularly
annoyed about it because that horribly slow Mr.
Mainwaring was there. He is as rich as Crœsus,
and mamma wanted me to marry him. But the

evening crowned the day.   I was in wild spirits,
and danced all night with Harry, and finally sat
for a full half-hour alone with him in that recess
where I had the pleasure of seeing you with Mr.
Lyne.   You can guess what tale it was that I
listened to there, and what my answer was.   In
an evil moment mamma passed by and gave me a
look of thunder.   I saw that a storm was gathering, and hoping to avert it, I told Harry that I
would not dance with him any more that night,
and that he must not attempt to speak to mamma
until I gave him leave to do so, for I dreaded that
she would 'cut up rough.'   He didn't seem to
like it.   However, he was obliged to give me the
required promise.   No sooner were all the people
gone than I got the most tremendous scolding
that a poor mortal could have. I was peremptorily
told that Mr. Caulfield was not a fit match for me,
and that, therefore, the way in which I flirted
with him was disgraceful, and, in fine, that there
must be an end to it.   I was in despair; but
thought that I had better let the squall blow over
and try to get Mary on my side.   Mary behaved
like an angel.   She saw that I really loved Harry,
and so she did all she could to let us meet as often
as possible, and in the meantime endeavoured to
influence mamma in his favour.   Thus things
went on as long as we remained in Rome, and for

some time after we got to Naples. At last, one
evening—by the way, Mr. Earnscliffe dined with
us on that day—a bouquet girl came to the door
ostensibly to sell bouquets, but in reality to bring
me a note from Harry. The note was to tell me
that he had just received a letter announcing
his sister's approaching marriage with an
officer about to start for India immediately,
and whose wedding must therefore take
place at once; but Harry declared that he
would either take me with him as his bride, or
never see me again. His note, I assure you,
Flora, was quite in the *romance* style, calling
upon me to choose between the man whom I professed to love, and a cruel, unreasonable parent.
He concluded by saying that he *had* waited
months in the hope of her relenting, and that he
would wait no longer, but on the next day would
formally ask mamma for my hand, and if she
refused her consent, it would remain with me to
decide between them. There was no possibility
of stopping him, for I could not write then, and
afterwards it would have been too late; but, to
say the truth, I did not want to do so. I was
getting heartily tired of manœuvring to see him,
and to keep mamma from forbidding me to speak
to him, so I was almost glad that it had come to
a crisis. The next day up came the hero, and

he was shown into the drawing-room, where Mary
and I were sitting in fear and trembling at the
coming attack on the citadel. Harry looked
awfully determined and braced up to the fighting
point as he came in, and walking up to Mary, he
said, ' Miss Elton, you are probably aware of what
my object in coming here to-day is, and I hope I
may count upon your seconding it.' Mary bowed,
and then he asked, ' Can I see Mrs. Elton ? ' ' I
will go and tell her that you are here,' answered
Mary. Harry had only time to say a few words
to me, when mamma came down, followed by
Mary. Then commenced the battle in earnest.
Everything that mamma said was bitter and cutting, and I, of course, was crying like a fool. At
last she concluded by saying, ' Mr. Caulfield, I
told Helena long ago that I disapproved of her
flirtation, as I would never give my consent to
her marriage with you, and I tell it to you now.
My consent she shall never have. She has braved
my displeasure hitherto, and I suppose she will
continue to do so. I have not the power to prevent her from becoming your wife if she chooses
to do it in spite of my prohibition ; but if she
does I will not give her any fortune whatsoever.'
The brightest of smiles played over Harry's face
as he replied, eagerly, ' As for the fortune, Mrs.
Elton, it is a matter of indifference to me. If

Helena can be satisfied to marry a comparatively poor man it's all right. I shall only regret her not having a fortune for her own sake. What do you say, Helena?' My answer was to go and place my hand in his, and he put his arm round my waist, saying, 'It's all right, you see, Mrs. Elton.' I saw mamma's eyes fill with tears, and pushing Harry away, I went and threw myself at her feet, and begged of her only to say that she would not be angry with me if I married him. I said that I did not want any money, but that I could not bear her displeasure. Mary came to the rescue, and joined her prayers to mine, and we wrung from mamma a sort of half consent, which Harry gladly seized on, and rushed off to the English chaplain to get everything arranged as quickly as possible. A fortnight after we were privately married. Mary was my only bridesmaid, and Mr. Lyne Harry's bridesman. Poor Mary looked heart-broken as she wished me good-bye, and I was so sorry to leave her; but I could not help wanting to go with Harry"—(Flora smiled)— " We travelled post-haste to Rome, intending to sail from Civita Vecchia; but at his banker's in Rome Harry found a letter from his sister, informing him that her marriage was put off for a few weeks, as her future husband's regiment was not to sail so soon as they had expected. How Harry

laughed when he got that letter, declaring that
if his sister had been playing into his hands, she
could not have helped him better to his wife, and
that he was sure if he had not taken mamma by
storm and carried me off in a whirlwind, he would
never have got me at all. We had now time to spare,
and I proposed that we should come here, as we had
neither of us seen Munich, and go home by the
Rhine. There's the end of my story; but, tell
me, wasn't it grand of Harry not to care about
my fortune when, naturally, he must have expected
that I would have a large one? And mamma
kept to it. She did not give me anything. But
Harry is such a darling, Flora, you can't think!"

"Take care, Helena; you are yet too young a
wife to sing your husband's praises. . . . Wait a
little."

"As if Harry would change, indeed!"

"Well, I don't at all mean to say that he will;
I only said that you must wait a while before
you gain the right of singing his praises. But
here we are at your hotel, for I see them all
standing at the door waiting for us."

"Yes, we are staying at the Bayrischer Hof,
—and you?"

"At the Vier Jahreszeiten; but we shall meet
at the theatre."

"Oh yes, we must spend this evening together,

for I heard Mrs. Adair say that you were going
away to-morrow; and I am not at all satisfied
about Mr. Earnscliffe; I must try and pick his
brains—or rather it is his heart that I want to
pick—to-night at the theatre. As you are so
close to it, suppose we call for you, and then we
can all go in together."

" Yes, that will be the better plan; then please
to be with us at a few minutes before six."

As they came up Mr. Caulfield said, looking
admiringly at Helena's bright laughing face,
" What a chatterbox my wife is, is she not, Miss
Adair ? "

"Not worse than her husband, at all events,"
answered Helena, taking his arm and pinching
it. She then wished her friends good-bye, until
six, promising for herself and Harry to be
punctual.

We may imagine what success Helena had
that evening in gleaning information from Mr.
Earnscliffe about the state of his heart; and the
next morning the Adair party were in the train
en route for Paris before the Caulfields had
finished their rather late breakfast.

CHAPTER V.

WHEN the Adairs arrived in Paris they found a letter waiting for them from Madame de St. Severan, stating that most unfortunately Monsieur de St. Severan had got a violent attack of the gout, which it was feared would detain him for some weeks at his chateau in the south, where they then were; therefore, to their deep regret, they were forced to give up the pleasure of going to Paris to receive their dear child Marie, and to thank her kind friends who had taken such care of her. But if Mrs. Adair would kindly write and say on what day Marie would be ready to leave Paris, they would send up a faithful old servant to take charge of her to the chateau. The letter concluded with a warm invitation to the Adairs to spend some time with them as soon as Monsieur de St. Severan should be recovered. Flora declared that Marie must not go away before her wedding, but the difficulty was how to get leave from the de St. Severans for her to stay,

without giving the true reason, for Flora did not
wish them to be told of her marriage; she said it
would be time enough to tell them just before it
took place,—it was so disagreeable to have a thing
of that kind spoken of beforehand. So Mrs.
Adair could only write to Madame de St. Severan
begging her to allow Marie to stay with them
until after the 21st, when they intended to leave
France, and holding out a hope that if the de St.
Severans were not able to come to Paris, then she
would take Marie to them herself. Mrs. Adair
pressed so earnestly for consent to this arrangement that it was granted, although somewhat
reluctantly, as Colonel de St. Severan was all
impatience to see Marie; however, the consent
was given, and Marie remained—for the wedding.

For nearly the first three weeks of their stay
in Paris Mr. Earnscliffe was in England, and,
notwithstanding her occupation—one too in which
ladies are supposed to take such delight, that of
getting her *trousseau*—Flora found the time pass
very slowly, and voted the *trousseau* a bore.
Marie, however, supplied for the bride elect's
abstraction, and superintended all its most minute
details.

Towards dusk one evening Flora sat in the
drawing-room window totally heedless of repeated
calls from Marie to come and see what pretty

things they were planning for her; but she sat
immovable in the half-dark silent room, whilst
from the one next to it there came a streak of
light and the sound of shrill French voices in full
chatter. Suddenly she started up and ran to the
outer door of their apartment, which she opened
as if by chance just as a gentleman was about to
ring at it. It was too dark for him to see who
the person was who opened it, particularly as she
stood very much behind it, and he asked in a
quick, eager tone, "*Madame Adair, est-elle chez
elle?*"

"*Est-ce bien Madame que Monsieur veut voir?*"
was the reply, in an odd muffled voice.

"*Les dames enfin,*" he returned, impatiently,
"*sont elles à la maison? Dites moi donc vite.*"

A low laugh was now the only answer, but it
seemed to satisfy Mr. Earnscliffe perfectly as to
whether the *ladies* were at home, for he did not
repeat his question, but caught the respondent in
his arms, and murmured between kisses, "Wicked
Flora! to try my patience so, and keep me waiting
for *this.*"

Now time resumed its gallop for Flora, and
everything became interesting. Being asked to
decide between this dress or that was no longer
tiresome, since Mr. Earnscliffe was there to
say which he thought the prettier. It came to

within about ten days of the eventful twenty-first, and everything seemed to bid fair to contradict the old saying that "the course of true love never did run smooth." But one evening as they drove home from the Bois de Boulogne, Mrs. Elton and Mary passed them, driving very fast, but not before Mary had time to recognise them and bow most markedly.

"The Eltons here!" exclaimed Flora. "Helena did not tell me that they were coming to Paris." And she looked at Mr. Earnscliffe, but to her amazement she saw that he had become strangely pale, and seemed scarcely to hear her; then, with that sort of shudder which she had before observed, he said, "Here! yes, I had no idea of it."

He scarcely spoke again all the evening, yet he could not bear Flora to be away from him for a moment.

Here was the first shadow: it was not a very great one, but it *was* one. Flora could no longer blind herself to the fact that in Mr. Earnscliffe's mind there was some sinister train of thought in connection with Mary Elton. To doubt Mr. Earnscliffe was an impossibility to her, and she only wished to know what it was that caused this gloom, whenever Mary Elton was named or seen, in order that she might better know how to cheer him and make him forget it. She could not speak to him on this subject, because, as he had not volunteered to tell her, any questioning or remarks upon it might look like distrust, and she could not bear to say anything which might wear the faintest semblance of such a feeling. So on that evening she could only exert all her powers of charm and affection to try to chase away his sadness. He stayed late, and when he was going away he held her for a moment longer than usual in his arms, and said, but more to himself than to her, " Would that you were really mine, Flora! then I should have nothing to dread, but now——"

" What is that you dread now, Edwin ? "

" You would laugh at me if I were to tell you, Flora, and it does seem to be folly, but—oh, the power of a woman for good or evil is fearful! I have a right to dread it."

" But tell me what it is that makes you sad, be it folly or not, and I will try to banish it away, Edwin," she said with a smile.

" That you would, darling, but I *must* not tell you. I am bound in honour not to do so, and you gave me so good an example some time ago on this point, that I should be unpardonable if I were to say a word. But you will trust me."

" Trust you, Edwin! " and her blue eyes, as they rested full on his face, looked worlds of trust.

"My own dearest, good-night!" and he gave
her the last kiss, adding, with a smile, as he turned
away, "I must not stay any longer, or you would
tempt me into telling you my foolish fears, to
have them *petted*—which would be better far
than reasoned—away."

But Mary Elton : what were her feelings on
thus seeing Mr. Earnscliffe driving in the carriage
with her rival? In order to understand them
fully, let us go back to that evening at Naples,
when, worked up to the highest pitch of excitement, she forgot all maidenly reserve, and allowed
Mr. Earnscliffe to see her ungovernable passion
for himself, and almost cursed Flora Adair. We
remember that she rushed away from him down
a side walk, as she heard the sound of an
approaching step ; but we did not see her a
moment later, when, coming to a stone bench,
she threw herself on the ground beside it, and
pressed her burning face upon its cool surface.
Suddenly, however, she felt something flowing
into her mouth, and raising her head, a stream of
blood came from her lips. She tried to stop it
with her handkerchief, and with her other hand
she clung to the bench for support, for everything
seemed to swim round her.

Thus Helena found her, and she started back
with fright as she saw her face, hands, and hand-

kerchief all besmeared with blood; then putting her arms round her, she made her lean against her as she exclaimed, " Oh, sister, what is the matter ? What can I do for you ? Shall I call any one ? "

Mary leaned her head heavily on Helena's shoulder, as if to keep her from moving, and half opened her closed eyes. Helena saw and understood well why it was so—that Mary did not wish any one to see her in this state; so Helena tried to remain quiet, but she felt so frightened about Mary, and so powerless to do or to get anything for her, being afraid to leave her, that she fairly broke down and began to cry. It roused Mary, however, for as Helena's tears fell like rain-drops on her face, she opened her eyes and tried to say, "It is nothing, I shall be better in a few minutes;" and again, after a moment's pause, she whispered, " Let me lean against the seat, and you go and dip your hand-kerchief in the fountain and bring it back to me."

"But I am afraid to leave you, Mary, dar-ling ! "

" Do not be afraid, go—oh, go ! "

Helena did not venture to hesitate any longer, for fear of irritating Mary and making her worse, so she settled her as comfortably as she could against the bench, went to the fountain, saturated her handkerchief well with cold water, and ran back with it to Mary, who muttered, "Put it upon my head." As Helena did so, Mary gave a deep drawn sigh of relief, then taking the wet handkerchief in her own hand, she rubbed it upon her face.

"Let me do it for you, Mary," said Helena, and she took the handkerchief from her and tried to remove the blood stains from Mary's lips, whilst the latter said, in a stronger voice than she had yet spoken, "Do you think you could take me up, Helena, and help me to the fountain. If I could only get to it I should be all right."

"I will try," answered Helena, and after a little time she did get her up; and holding her tightly round the waist, and with Mary's arm thrown across her shoulders, they at last got to the fountain. Mary plunged her hands into the cold water, deluged her face with it, and repeated this process until all feeling of faintness was gone. Helena stood by, watching her mournfully, until at length Mary said, "There, now it's all over, and so don't look frightened any more, Lena."

"But, Mary, what was all that blood? You have not burst a blood-vessel, surely!"

"Nonsense, child," said Mary, quickly, although in her heart she thought that what Helena said was true, that she had burst a blood-vessel; "I probably hurt myself against the bench, and my nose and mouth bled."

"I hope it was only that, dear sister; and now please, please to believe that I did not willingly disobey you about Flora. He found it out, Mary, before I knew what I was saying,—forgive me, forgive me," and Helena knelt before Mary.

"Helena!" Mary almost screamed, "never again dare to mention that subject to me, the past is buried, and"—with bitterness—"washed away in my blood. None know it but you, and none ever can know it but *through* you; be silent as the grave upon it to me as well as to others! Lena"—her voice changed and lost all its sternness—"do not thwart me by ever alluding to it; you are all that is left to me to love now. Speak to me of yourself—of how I can help you—and I shall be glad to have anything good to do or to think about."

Helena kissed her fondly, and thinking that, as she herself said, it would be well for her to have something to do and to think about, she put Mr. Caulfield's letter into her hand. Mary read it by the moonlight, which, as we may recollect, was very bright that night. Then she said, "We must go in now; I will go upstairs and change my dress, and you can tell mamma that I have gone to do so, as I got it wet by sitting at the fountain; that is true, heaven knows." She held up her arms, and the water dripped from her light muslin sleeves.

The first thing that Mary did on getting to her own room was to drink off about twenty drops of sal-volatile, in the smallest possible quantity of water—she had latterly given herself the habit of taking these stimulants—and then as soon as she had changed her dress, and carefully folded up and put away the blood-stained one, together with her own and Helena's handkerchief, she went down-stairs, and appeared to be very much as usual for the remainder of the evening. Then next day, as we already know, began all the fuss and hurry about Helena's marriage, and for the ensuing fortnight excitement kept Mary up. But on the evening of Helena's wedding day, after the bridal party had left, as Mary sat before the dressing-table to have her hair arranged for dinner, the maid saw even in the glass that she suddenly changed countenance, and her lips formed the word " basin " although scarcely any sound came from them. She handed it to her with all possible speed, and again the blood streamed from Mary's lips. The maid was able to reach the bell from where she stood at the dressing-table, and rang it violently. The house was soon in commotion, and Mrs. Elton, though evidently much agitated, was the only one who preserved any presence of mind. Without a moment's delay, she sent off a messenger to their doctor, and in case that he should not be at home, she desired the former not to return without some good medical man; and having done this, she turned all her attention to trying to get Mary stretched upon her bed, as she was sure that she would be better if she could be laid on her back. They succeeded in this, and the vomiting of blood ceased for the time being.

Dr. Danvers, their regular physician, came quickly on the receipt of Mrs. Elton's urgent message. Almost immediately after seeing Mary he said that she had burst a blood-vessel from over excitement, but that as far as he could judge at present there was not any danger if she could be kept perfectly quiet. Mrs. Elton of course promised that this should be done, and Dr. Danvers, having written a prescription, and given all necessary directions for the night, took his leave, saying that he would see the patient early next morning.

The first words which Mary spoke were, "Mamma, remember, you must not say that I am ill when you write to Lena,—promise me this faithfully, or I shall have no rest."

"Of course I will promise it, dear child,"

answered Mrs. Elton ; "everything shall be done that you wish, only keep yourself quiet, and then you will soon be well again. I never supposed that Lena's leaving us would be such a blow to you, and yet how you urged on that marriage for her sake. How unselfishly you must love her, Mary."

Mary's eyes filled with tears, and her mother, dreading any agitation for her, kissed her and went away. Mary now progressed slowly but steadily from day to day, and before long she was able to go about again. But when Dr. Danvers was taking his final leave of her he said significantly, "Young lady, beware of violent excitement. To break a blood-vessel about the heart a second time is most dangerous, a third time fatal. In persons of your temperament feeling should be given way to naturally, and not hidden and pent up in their own hearts, for then it swells and swells until it bursts, and inundations, we all know, sometimes destroy life. Remember my words, young lady, if you would be long-lived. And now allow me to wish you good-bye, and at the same time health and happiness."

Dr. Danvers might have spared his advice. There could be no natural outlet for that secret passion which Mary kept "pent up" indeed in her own heart. She burned to know where Mr.

Earnscliffe and Flora Adair—for she never doubted that they were together—were, and what was the result of their meeting. Suddenly it occurred to her that perhaps they were in Paris. She remembered that the Adairs had said in Rome that they expected to get to Paris by the end of May. It was the first of June now, so in all probability they were there, and Mary resolved that she and Mrs Elton should go too, murmuring at the same time, "I told him to dread me in the hour when he felt most sure of Flora Adair. For her he slighted my love, and I will snatch her from him yet—how, I know not—but I will do it or die."

Helena had not ventured to tell Mary that she met the Adairs and Mr. Earnscliffe in Munich, so it was on chance that Mary determined upon inducing her mother to go to Paris, and Mrs. Elton at once consented, not wishing to oppose Mary in anything just after her illness. Accordingly they arrived in Paris a day or two before that evening when they met the Adairs and Mr. Earnscliffe in the Champs Elysées.

Mary had expected to see them together, yet the realisation of what she expected was a shock to her. A sharp pain shot across her heart, and tears of rage and jealousy started to her eyes, but, heedless of Dr. Danvers' parting admonition, she forced them back, and exerted herself to appear unconcerned, and when she retired to her own room for the night, she did not go to bed, but sat pale and exhausted in an armchair, meditating upon what she could do to separate them. "I saw him start as he caught sight of me, so he has not forgotten that night at Naples, and it shall be recalled still more forcibly to his memory before long,—yet how? I do not even know where either he or the Adairs are staying; however that I can find out. What then? Oh, that I were Iago to his Othello! Heavens! it is not possible that they are married and that I am too late!" she exclaimed, springing from her chair. "No, no, it cannot be, I should have heard of it; but even if they are, I am not too late,—revenge is still possible, only let me have the means! But it is of no use to think any more to-night; to-morrow I must find out where they are, and then —now, oh give me rest, rest!"

The next morning she sent their courier to the police to inquire where a Madame et Mademoiselle Adair et Mademoiselle Arbi were residing, and desired him to be shown up to her room the instant he came back. . . . She trembled as she heard his step approach, and it had seemed like ages to her until his knock came to the door. "*Entrez*," she cried eagerly. He went in and gave

her an answer, for which he received a most earnest
"*Merci beaucoup.*" The answer was that the *three*
ladies were residing in an apartment in the
Avenue de Marigny, 29. "Now," thought Mary,
"we can go and call upon them, and there we
shall hear where Mr. Earnscliffe is. So far all is
well; I am still in time to keep my word to him.
We had better go early to the Adairs—about
half-past one—so as to catch them at home; so I
must go and tell mamma, as it must be long past
twelve now." She entered the drawing-room,
where Mrs. Elton was sitting reading, and was
just going to propose the visit to the Adairs,
when Thomas opened the door and announced
"Mr. Maunsell."

Mary frowned with displeasure, for she feared
that the visitor—she could not think of any one
whom she knew of that name—might make them
late in going to the Adairs, and she felt indignant
with Thomas for allowing any one to come in at
such an undue hour for visitors—"before one
o'clock—preposterous!" But Mrs. Elton exclaimed, with a bright smile, as a venerable-
looking, grey-haired old gentleman came in, "Mr.
Maunsell, how delighted I am to see you!"

Mary saw with surprise that her mother's eyes
were swimming in tears, and the old gentleman,
whom she was sure *she* had never seen before,

kept her hand in his as he said, "Poor William! You and he were together when last I saw you."

They both remained silent for a second or two, and then Mrs. Elton said, "Mary, come and make the acquaintance of an old friend of your dear father's. You have heard me speak of Mr. Maunsell often, and of having stayed at his country seat, near Earnscliffe Court, years ago."

As if by magic Mary's frown vanished, and her whole face lit up; even Mrs. Elton was astonished at the singular graciousness of her manner as she expressed her pleasure at being introduced to Mr. Maunsell; yet she was much gratified by it, for she looked upon it as a proof of how dear her father's memory was to Mary; and Mr. Maunsell seemed to be quite touched as he said, "Thank you, my dear, for receiving me so warmly; we old people value cordiality from the young so much."

But neither of them had got the right key to her sudden change of manner,—that key was the word Earnscliffe Court. "He must know Mr. Earnscliffe then," she thought, "and possibly he might be of some use to her—who could tell?"

When they were all seated Mrs. Elton said, "How did you know that we were in Paris, Mr. Maunsell?"

"Well, by the merest chance," he answered. "I met Earnscliffe unexpectedly—I did not know that he was here, either—and in the course of conversation I asked him if he knew you, adding that you and his parents had been intimate friends. He said he had met you in Italy, and then I asked him if he had any idea where you were now; he answered, somewhat abruptly I thought, 'I suppose they are here, for I saw them driving in the Champs Elysées last evening, but I know nothing more about them.' I did not like to lose the chance of seeing you, without making some exertion, and accordingly I went to Galignani, in hopes of finding your address, and as you see, I was successful."

"It was so good of you to take the trouble of finding us out."

"It was not goodness, my dear; I felt that it would be a gratification, even if a sad one, to me to see you again. But come, I must not make you think of bygones," he added, as he saw Mrs. Elton's eyes beginning to glisten again; "let us talk of something cheering. By the way, I think Earnscliffe is going to be married again."

Mary felt as if the beating of her heart stood still, as Mrs. Elton exclaimed, "Again! Why, has he been married? Is he a widower?"

"Married! to be sure he has been, but he is

only a widower in law," answered Mr. Maunsell with a smile.

Mary could stay quiet no longer; she stood up and went to the window, apparently to arrange the blind, and then seated herself so that the shadow of the curtain fell upon her.

"What do you mean?" asked Mrs. Elton. "We have resided so much out of England for the last twelve years, that I know nothing of all this. Do tell us the whole history."

Mr. Maunsell, who enjoyed telling a story, acceded to this request with the utmost willingness.

"It must be somewhat more than ten years ago now, I should say, since the beautiful Miss Foster was the reigning belle in London. Mr. Foster had been lavishly extravagant all his life, and it was generally known that he depended upon his only child's making a rich marriage in order to stave off absolute ruin. If beauty can be called a fortune, Amelia Foster certainly had an ample dower. Well, in the beginning of the season Earnscliffe was abroad, but towards its close he returned to London, and was, of course, introduced to Miss Foster. From the first moment that he laid eyes upon her he was a doomed man, and by the end of the season he had proposed and was accepted. Old Foster was in a high state of

triumph at having secured *such* a son-in-law. He
thought that there was nothing which he might not
expect from Earnscliffe, with his lordly possessions
and well-known generosity ; but it was observed
by more than one that the young lady looked sad
and dejected from the time of his proposal. She
pleaded hard, I am told, not to be married until
after her next birthday, which was some months
off. Earnscliffe chafed at so long an engagement ;
but he could not refuse her anything that she chose
to ask for. I never saw a man more bewitched
by a woman than he was, and she tried him
pretty well. Her worst prank was insisting on
fulfilling a promise which she had made to go on
a tour with her uncle's family through Switzerland
and Germany. I used to see a good deal of him
at the time, and although it was evident how
much this tour annoyed him, he would not allow
any one to find fault with her. Accordingly, she
went off with her Uncle and Aunt Stanly, and
her two cousins, John and Alfred. John was the
eldest son, and a quiet ordinary young man ; but
Alfred was a handsome, gay, wild fellow, and it
was whispered that if he and Earnscliffe could
have changed places with regard to the fair
Amelia, she would not have wanted to see Switzerland just then. No one, however, ventured to
say this to Earnscliffe. You know it is not easy

to take any liberty with him. Poor fellow ! he spent the time of her absence all alone at Earnscliffe Court, superintending the adorning of it for its future mistress. At last, late in October, she came back. I was not in London then ; but I heard from friends there that Miss Foster looked wretchedly ill. However, she did not complain, and there was no further postponement of the marriage, and it was celebrated on the 20th of November. I remember the date well, for it was the day upon which I myself was married. And on that very day Alfred Stanly received the official announcement that he was nominated to a place in the Home Department of the Foreign Office, which Earnscliffe had procured for him. I was one of the wedding guests, I went up to London especially for it, and I heard the Stanlys showering thanks upon Earnscliffe for his kindness to Alfred as they took leave of him, and he led his bride to the carriage. They spent three weeks or so in the south of England, and then they came to Earnscliffe Court for Christmas, which was to be kept there with grand festivities. The house was full of company, and among others was Alfred Stanly, who had just passed his examination for his new appointment. He was a clever fellow enough when he chose to exert himself. Everything went off to perfection, and the

bride was at times lively and charming ; at others
silent and abstracted; I often saw Earnscliffe
look at her with a melancholy puzzled air. At
length all the guests went away except Alfred
Stanly, who was to remain with them until the
middle of January, when he was to begin his
attendance at the office. One day I met them out
driving, and Earnscliffe told me that he was
going to London that evening on business; but
Mrs. Earnscliffe exclaimed eagerly, 'Oh, Mr.
Maunsell, you have influence with my husband—
do try and persuade him not to go now. He
might as well wait for Alfred, who will be going
to town in a fortnight, and they could go together !' I was going to try what I could do to
forward her wishes, but Earnscliffe said gravely,
'Do you suppose, Amelia, that I would stay at
home at the request of another, when I thought
it right to refuse you ? I really must go at once ;
but I shall be back in a week.' 'A week !' she
repeated, and I shall never forget the scared expression of her face : but she said no more. And
I thought nothing further about them until five
or six days afterwards, when the rumours spread
through the country that late on the previous
night Earnscliffe had returned unexpectedly, but
quitted his house not half an hour after he had
entered it, drove back to the railway station, and

took the night mail up to London, and also that
Mrs. Earnscliffe and Stanly left early next morning. The next thing we heard was that Earnscliffe had sued for and obtained a divorce, and
that his unfortunate wife had become Mrs. Alfred
Stanly. This morning was the first time since
that dreadful affair that Earnscliffe and I have
met."

"Why, you have told us quite a romance,"
exclaimed Mrs. Elton; but she was prevented
from saying anything more by Mary's getting a
violent fit of coughing: she made a sign to her,
however, not to mind her, and with her handkerchief pressed to her mouth she stood up and
left the room.

"Miss Elton is not ill, I hope?" said Mr.
Maunsell.

"Oh no!" answered Mrs. Elton; "she will probably be all right again in a moment. And now
I will ring for luncheon. You must not run away
from us until after that, at all events."

Mr. Maunsell allowed himself to be prevailed
upon to stay for it, and after a little time they
repaired to the dining-room, where Mary joined
them, looking very pale, but her eyes sparkled
brilliantly, and as she came into the room she
said, "I was sorry that my tiresome cough
obliged me to leave you just as you finished your

interesting story, Mr. Maunsell; but you said that you thought Mr. Earnscliffe was going to marry again. And who is to be his second bride?"

"That I can't tell you; for, as you may imagine, marriage is the last subject in the world upon which *I* can speak to him. But I suppose he is going to be married, because Earnscliffe Court is being all refurnished, and I know that he was in England some time ago, and was very much with his lawyers,—that looks like settlements. Then he told me to-day that he was going with some ladies to the grand ball at the Hotel de Ville, given for charity, which is to be to-morrow night."

"Going to the ball, is he, with her?" said Mary, and she laughed a low, strange laugh; then added suddenly, "Mr. Maunsell will you escort us to it? They say it will be a grand sight!"

"Surely I am too old for going to balls, my dear!"

"Indeed you are not, and I want you to come with us," answered Mary, with her sweetest smile. "Now you must not refuse the first request of my father's daughter."

"So you have already found out the way to make me do what you like!"

" Then you will come ?   Oh, thank you ! "

" And you must come and dine with us," said Mrs. Elton ; " then we can go late to the ball."

" Of course I cannot refuse *you* after granting my young friend's less congenial request.   At what hour do you dine ?"

" Our usual hour is seven."

" Then I shall not fail to be with you by that time."

CHAPTER VI.

Soon after Mr. Maunsell left them, and Mrs. Elton said, "Really, Mary, I am quite uneasy about you; you look dreadfully flushed and excited, and that fit of coughing was almost convulsive. I must take you to Dr. O——; and I do not think that I can allow you to go to the ball. I did not like to oppose you while Mr. Maunsell was here, but now that we are alone, I am sure that I have only to appeal to your own good sense in order to induce you to give it up, especially as I know that you do not care about balls."

"But I *do* care about this one," cried Mary eagerly—however, she continued in a calmer tone as she saw her mother look at her in amazement —"and please to let me go to it; afterwards I will see any doctor you choose. This ball is the first amusement that I have felt a wish to partake of since Lena's marriage, and to prevent me from going to it will only be a new cause of irritation."

"Well, I suppose it is the lesser of two evils to let you go, since you have set your heart upon it; but why is it so? You never liked balls before. There is something altogether strange about you—something that I do not understand, and that your grief for Lena does not account for; that would not make your cheeks flush, nor your eyes flash as they do now. What is the cause of it all, Mary?"

"God knows! Derangement of the nervous system, I suppose. But talking about it, mamma, can do no good; it can only increase the evil. Wait till the ball is over, and then try what doctors can do for me," answered Mary gloomily, as she hastily left the room.

Poor Mrs. Elton was sadly perplexed. She saw that there was some secret influence at work within Mary's heart, yet she feared to question her any farther, as it seemed to increase her excitement so much, and in vain she tried to form any *clear* idea of its cause. A faint suspicion crossed her mind that Mr. Earnscliffe had something to do with it; and as she thought over the events of the last few weeks it struck her that since that day when he dined with them at Naples Mary had never been quite herself, and this wild desire to go to the ball, after she heard that he was to be there, seemed to corroborate it all.

The result of these meditations was to render
Mrs. Elton sad, and thoughtfully serious, as she
said to herself, " Since William's death, I have
had no thought on earth but to make my children
happy and prosperous in the world, yet I do not
appear to have succeeded. Lena has made a poor
match, in opposition to my wishes, and Mary has
some secret sorrow preying on her; yet how
carefully I trained them to avoid all romance and
love nonsense, and I thought at one time that
Mary, at least, was a model of sense and discretion; but I fear it is impossible to think so any
more. Can my teaching have been false? Oh,
my children, do not make me feel that I have
been to blame in your regard,—you for whom
alone I have lived through these long twelve
years of widowhood!" Then with a sigh she,
stood up, and went to Mary's room to ask her
what she would like to do for the afternoon.

"To drive," was Mary's laconic answer. She
had evidently given up the projected visit to the
Adairs. And well she might; for there was
nothing to be gained from it now. The tale
which Mr. Maunsell had told was to her as
if she had been suddenly shown a mine of gunpowder, over which her victims were unconsciously
walking. She felt that she had but to apply the
match to it in order to blast their happiness to

atoms ; and she revelled in this coming triumph
of her revenge. Her excitement was almost un-
controllable ; it was killing her by inches, and she
knew it ; but she could not relinquish her triumph.
Come what would, she must go to the ball and
fire the mine ; after that she resolved to give herself up altogether into the hands of a doctor, and
perhaps, even then, she thought it might still be
time to save her life.

Mary, having so many Catholic relations, knew
—what Mr. Earnscliffe did not—that Flora Adair,
according to her religion, must look upon a man
who had got a divorce, but whose wife was still
living, as a married man. Therefore it was that
Mr. Maunsell's revelations filled her heart with
such savage delight. She pictured to herself
Flora's misery on hearing it ; her struggles
between love and religion ; Mr. Earnscliffe's
entreaties, reproaches, and final despair and
indignation ; and she laughed bitterly as she
thought over each detail of the suffering which
she was about to inflict. And if she could only
make Flora believe that Mr. Earnscliffe had
intended to deceive her,—to marry her, although
he knew from the first that it would be no
marriage to her,—then, indeed, would her revenge
be complete.

The eventful night arrived. But when Mary

went up to dress she felt so ill that she could scarcely stand, and as she sighed heavily her mouth became full of blood. She spat it out hurriedly, and taking a bottle of lavender drops, she put it to her lips, and held it there until she felt herself reviving. She then put it down and corked it up, saying, "I hope to-morrow will not be too late to see Dr. O———. But too late or not, I cannot help it now; I must go on and take my chance for the rest." She rang for her maid, and began to dress.

When she went into the drawing-room in her flowing white dress, covered with light gauzy blue draperies, old as he was, Mr. Maunsell looked at her admiringly, and said, "You are as good, my dear, I hope, as you are handsome."

"But I am not, Mr. Maunsell," she answered impetuously; and her voice trembled, for his words affected her strangely, and she did not speak again until they were in the midst of that most brilliant of sights—a ball at the Hotel de Ville in Paris; its vast *salles* one blaze of light, which together with the fountains, trees, and flowers, formed a scene of fairy-like splendour.

The Eltons had not been there much more than a quarter of an hour when the Adair party arrived, with Mr. Earnscliffe, and another gentleman

whom Mary did not know. Mrs. Adair was leaning upon the strange gentleman's arm, and the two
girls followed with Mr. Earnscliffe. Mary longed
to pounce upon her prey ; but she considered that
it would be wiser to defer the final stroke until
she could get Flora separated from the others.
However, she might go and speak to them at
once ; so she said, " Mamma, there are the Adairs.
Shall we go and join them ?"

" If you like, dear," answered Mrs. Elton, watching her narrowly to try and discover if Mr. Earnscliffe had really anything to do with her feverish
state of excitement. And when they got to the
Adairs she did imagine that she saw Mary's hand
tremble as she shook hands with him, whilst he
scarcely touched hers. Mrs. Elton felt convinced
that there was some mystery connected with him,
and resolved to speak to Mary gravely about it
to-morrow. She was so occupied with her own
thoughts that she scarcely noticed Mrs. Adair's
saying to her, " Allow me to introduce my son,
Mr. Adair, to you, Caroline."

She bowed half mechanically, but recollecting
herself, she said, " Oh, we must shake hands, Mr.
Adair. Your mother and I are old friends ; we
knew each other as girls. And here is my eldest
daughter, Mary. You have heard of her and her
sister Helena from Flora, I dare say."

" If he *has* not," thought Mary, as they shook hands, " he will hear of me from her. So he has come over for the wedding ! But he might have spared himself the trouble, I can tell him. There will be *no* wedding, or else his sister must abjure the errors of Popery ; but heaven forbid that she should do so, for then my revenge would be frustrated !" and her eyes glared on Flora.

Flora did not see that angry glance, but Mr. Earnscliffe did, and he could not bear it. He felt that he must get Flora away ; and turning abruptly to her he said, " May I have the pleasure of dancing with you, Miss Adair ?"

It was a valse ! Flora looked at him in astonishment, but took his offered arm ; and he led her away quickly into the crowd of dancers. Flora could not understand it. She knew that he seldom danced himself, and that he did not like her to valse ; therefore she had determined never to do so again, although *she* saw nothing objectionable in it. What, then, could have come over him to-night to make him propose dancing it with her himself ? And almost before she had time to recover from her astonishment he whirled her round and round at such a pace and holding her so tightly that she was quite out of breath when they stopped after a very few minutes of it. He piloted her out of the crush towards one of the

fountains, where they found a nice shady seat
close at hand, and she was very glad to sit down.
He stood before her, looking at her anxiously,
and said, "I fear I have tired you, Flora."

"Not tired me," she answered with a smile;
"but you have put me somewhat out of breath.
And now do tell me what made you dance to-
night? I thought you disliked dancing,—valsing
especially."

"Valsing is not disagreeable *sometimes*," he
returned gaily. "But the truth is that I wanted
to get you away from those people; and I could
think of no other way of doing it but by proposing to dance. How heated you look; where is
your fan?"

"I gave it to mamma to hold for me whilst I
arranged my necklace, just before you asked me
to dance."

"Then I will go and get it for you. I saw Mrs.
Adair sit down near to where we were standing."

"I do not want it, Edwin. Stay with me."

"Yes you do, dearest; you look so hot. I shall
be back in a moment;" and he hastened away.
But he would not have gone had he seen Mary
Elton approaching from the other side, leaning
on Mr. Maunsell.

"So here you are all alone, Flora," said Mary,
going up to her.

" Yes," replied Flora. " Mr. Earnscliffe has just left me to go and get my fan from mamma. I was heated after valsing."

" But, nevertheless, I dare say you enjoyed it with *such* a partner. And now let me wish you joy, Flora; I did not like to do it while there were so many by." Flora blushed, but made no answer, as she wondered how Mary had heard of her approaching marriage; and the latter continued, " But I did not know that you Catholics recognised the law of divorce, even for those who are not in your Church ? "

Flora felt a sensation of icy cold creeping over her as she asked with a gasp, " What do you mean, Mary ? "

" Why, of course Mr. Earnscliffe has told you that he was obliged to divorce his wife about two months after their marriage, and that she is still living, and the wife of his rival. Mr. Earnscliffe's friend here, Mr. Maunsell, knew *Mrs.* Earnscliffe very well."

Surely, even in this moment of her triumph, Mary must have felt a touch of pity as she saw poor Flora's eyes close, and large drops of perspiration burst out on her forehead; but with a supreme effort at self-control, Flora opened her eyes, and looking at Mary, said, " You were right when you supposed that we Catholics do not

recognise the law of divorce; but what this has to
do with Mr. Earnscliffe I can't see, for I have
never said, nor has he, that there was any engagement between us. Now, adieu for the present,"
and Flora turned away her head. Mary thought
she saw Mr. Earnscliffe coming, and not wishing
to meet him just then, she drew Mr. Maunsell
away, but looked back with an almost pitying
glance at Flora, and murmured to herself, "She
is a brave girl! How she tried to bear up in
order to save him from the imputation of having
deceived her! Yet the bare thought of it must
rankle in her heart. My revenge is working
well!"

Meanwhile, Flora was writhing under this
overwhelming blow. There was not a ray of
comfort for her on any side, and the javelin of
distrust which Mary had so cleverly barbed was
lacerating her heart, although she struggled with
all her might to cast it from her. But did not
this fatal disclosure clearly explain Mr. Earnscliffe's hitherto unaccountable dread of Mary
Elton? To know that she must either give up
him whom she loved, or her religion, was—heaven
knows!—torture enough; but it would be nothing
in comparison to being forced to believe him to be
unworthy of that love—a deceiver, in short; that
would be agony! and she exclaimed within

herself, " No, it is not so,—he is *true*, if heaven is true ! "

At this moment Mr. Earnscliffe returned with the fan, but as he saw Flora leaning back with closed eyes, and a look of terror in her face, he cried, as he threw himself on the seat beside her, " Flora, speak, are you ill ? What is the matter ? "

She looked at him earnestly, but did not answer; that look, however, was enough to make her feel, " Yes, he *is* true, and I cannot give him up."

" Flora, dearest," he called again, " answer me! What is the matter with you ? "

" The heat, or something, has been too much for me.   Take me home, Edwin," she said, in a low, plaintive voice.

" You must take something first—wine—champagne—what shall I get you ? "

" Oh, do not leave me again, Edwin ! "

" Flora," he exclaimed, " something has happened during my absence which has put you into this state; tell me what it is ? "

" How hot it is," she murmured, putting her hand to her forehead.

" Good God ! Flora, you are not going to faint, I hope." He stood up hastily—" Take my arm, and let us get out upon one of the balconies; the air will set you to rights."

She took his arm silently, and leaned heavily upon it, as she passively allowed him to lead her where he liked. As soon as they got to the balcony he put his arm round her waist, and said, " Now, my precious one, tell me, what is it all about ? "

She did feel a little revived, and it was so sweet to stand there in the cool night air, with his strong protecting arm round her; but how could she tell him what had happened ? Yet she must do it, if it were only to have her faith in his truth confirmed, so at last she said, " Mary Elton " —she felt his arm tremble; it made her start, and she asked, in a piteous tone of voice, " Edwin! what has made you dread Mary Elton ? "

" Go on, finish what you were going to tell me," was his only answer.

To obey him was like an instinct to Flora, and she began again timidly, " Mary Elton and a Mr. Maunsell—I think that was the name she said—came to me while you were away, and they began to talk of your—your marriage, long ago."

" Well, dearest, but why should this affect you so ? You remember, I told you all about it at

Achensee; how, a short time after I had obtained possession of one whom I believed to be a treasure, I discovered that she had betrayed me. Of course you understood that I got a divorce immediately; indeed, I told you that I put the case into the hands of my lawyers at once, and left England."

Flora forgot everything else in her wild joy at this perfect vindication of his truth, and she buried her face on his shoulder; but she was roused by his saying, as he placed his right hand on her head, " Darling, you have not yet told me what it was that so frightened you."

She shook all over as the sad reality was recalled to her, and his utter unconsciousness of what the fact of his first wife being still alive was to a Catholic, increased her pain, as she answered, " I have been very stupid, Edwin,—you did tell me everything of your past life, with your own truth and honour, but I misunderstood you. I thought that she of whom you spoke as having betrayed your love, was only your betrothed, not your wife, and—and—" she could get no further, and Mr. Earnscliffe said, quickly, " Flora, I don't understand you. What difference does that mistake make to you? Do you love me less because my misfortune has been deeper than even you supposed?"

" *Love* you less, Edwin !—more—more if it were possible, but—" the words came slowly, and with great agitation—" there is no—no such thing as divorce in the eyes of—of a Catholic !"

It was like an electric shock to him, and his voice trembled with emotion, as he cried, " But I was not married as a Catholic ; your laws cannot affect me ! Flora Adair, you are not going to give me up for this,—it can be but mere prejudice !"

Flora fell from his encircling arm on her knees to the ground beside him, murmuring, as she clasped his hands in her own, " Ask me nothing to-night,—I am bewildered and half maddened ; take me to mamma now, and to-morrow morning come to me and you shall know all. God help me !" and Flora moaned aloud.

" Flora," he cried again, raising her from the ground, " do you expect me to be able to pass the night in such suspense as this ? If you are half maddened now, what should I be by that time ? But here are people coming ; I must take you out of this place. Can I not see you to-night in your own house ?"

" No, Edwin, that cannot be, unless I tell mamma and my brother, and then perhaps they would never let me see you again. Do you wish me to tell them ? "

"No, no. I suppose it must be as you say. But if *you* fail me—oh, Flora, Flora!"

He said no more, but the agonised tone of his voice rang in Flora's ears with a dull, heavy, crushing sound, and she whispered—

"Take me to the cloak-room, and then go for mamma and the others. I shall escape observation better in that way. Tell mamma that I do not feel well."

Mr. Earnscliffe silently did as Flora desired, and before many minutes her party joined her; but Mr. Earnscliffe did not come with them. They got into their carriage and drove home. Flora hurriedly said good-night and went to her own room; and now that she was at last alone, and free from restraint, "all the winds" of passion did indeed

> "Leap forth, each hurtling each,
> Met in the wildness of a ghastly war,"

which was about to be waged in her heart. . . . Will she come forth from that war victorious, although wounded and heart-broken? or conquered and fallen? Will her one mainstay—her firm conviction in the truth and the divine authority of her religion—carry her triumphantly through it? or will she sink under the enemy's sharp blows from want of that child-like love and confidence in the goodness of God which would have blunted

their edge? Ah, who can tell? It is a fearful
test to be called upon to dash away the cup which
human happiness is "uplifting, pressing, and to
lips like" hers! Let us, then, follow her into her
room and watch the warfare's course.

She fastened the door, threw aside her cloak,
and tearing off her pearl necklace—a gift of Mr.
Earnscliffe's—as if its clasp round her neck were
choking her, she walked up and down the room
with rapid steps, and her hands nervously pressed
together. At last she exclaimed—

"Great God! it is as if Thou didst sport with
the heart of Thy creature! It would seem as if
it were to crush that heart with tenfold force that
Thou didst lead me through a youth of deep
yearning after some object worthy of devoting
myself to unreservedly, until I met one who filled
the void; and then after opening up to me a vista
of happiness and of a blessed work to be accom-
plished—that of healing his wounded spirit and
leading it to the knowledge of truth which it has
so long sought for in vain—Thou callest upon me
to give him up, and not only that, but at the same
time, with my own hand, to inflict on him a blow
which will cast him back into darkness and
despair! Is this love or justice?"

She stopped short in her quick walk, and stood
before the window gazing out on the now quiet,

deserted avenue, and then she raised her eyes
slowly to the blue starry sky above, as if, indeed,
she would cry with Promethus—

> "O majesty of earth, my solemn mother!
> . . . . Earth and Ether,
> Ye I invoke to know the wrongs I suffer."

With a groan she turned away, threw herself
upon a chair, and covered up her face with her
hands; but after a few minutes she took them
down, and said slowly—

"But let me try to think calmly. . . . Perhaps
I have been too hasty in at once supposing that I
must give him up.   Marriage, except among
Catholics, is not a sacrament : it is merely a civil
contract made by law, and 'what the law can
make it can break' is an old-established maxim,
therefore Edwin is evidently free."   She paused ;
but again she resumed her soliloquy.   "Yet the
Church, I know, does not recognise the law of
divorce even among those who are not her children ; but if that decree be against reason, justice,
and charity, am I bound to submit to it ?   It could
not be a good deed to drive him to despair, and
that, too, without being able to give him any suf-
ficiently sound reason—at least, any which would
appear so to him—for my conduct.   He would
think that my love for him was not strong
enough to make me give up—as he would call it—

a mere prejudice of my education. It would only make him hate, and keep him away from, religious truth. No, I cannot do this. There is no really good reason why I may not be your wife, my beloved, and that I will be ! So now it is decided, I will marry him ; and having begun the night in true heroine style, with a wild rhapsody, I had better finish it like a rational person and go to bed. But *how* I wish that he had never been married, or that she " (Flora gave her no name) " were dead ! "

She stood up, took off her ball dress, put on her dressing-gown, and began to take down her hair.

Has the battle, then, been fought and lost ? Is Flora about to fall from light to darkness ? Will she be false to her own principle ? Will she cast herself into the chaos of uncertainty and shifting opinion from which she would have drawn her lover ? Does she forget, when she says that her refusal to marry him would keep him away from religious truth, that if she does marry him, she places a stronger barrier than ever between him and it ? Yet stay, the battle is not quite over ; even if the enemy has gained possession of the colours for the moment, they may be regained by the poor combatant.

Flora had just finished unweaving the thick

plaits of her hair, when she impetuously dashed it back from off her face, exclaiming, as she resumed her pacing up and down the room—

"What sophistry all this is with which I have been endeavouring to satisfy myself! Religion declares that there can be no divorce but in death; and Edwin Earnscliffe's—ah!—wife lives! Therefore, it is vain to try to compromise between my religion and my love. I must choose between them; and, O God, what a choice! Fool that I was! I said that to refuse to marry him would keep him away from religious truth; but do I not know that to consent to it is to deny the principle of certainty, and to force him, even for my sake, to shut his eyes to truth? and thus I should be a curse instead of a blessing to him, not only in time, but in eternity. Edwin, I must bear your reproaches and your misery; but I cannot be a curse to you! No—no!" And she fell upon her knees before an ivory crucifix which stood on a little side table, murmuring, "My God! now teach me to do Thy will! . . . "

And there let us leave her to find strength and grace, whilst we return to the Hotel de Ville to see what has become of Mr. Earnscliffe.

When he left Flora in the cloak-room, he lost not a moment in seeking out Mrs. Adair, with whom, fortunately, he found her son and Marie,

so that there was no delay in looking for any of
the party, and they at once hastened down to
Flora. But Mr Earnscliffe had scarcely delivered
her message, when he felt his arm touched, and
turning round he saw Mary Elton standing beside
her mother, who was sitting talking to some ladies
near her.

"Mr. Earnscliffe," Mary said, in a low, impressive manner, " do you remember that I gave
you a rendezvous that night in Naples? I am
here to keep it now. Will you take me into the
refreshment-room ? "

But without waiting for an answer, she took
his arm. The touch of her hand was like the
sting of an adder to him. In common politeness,
however, he could not shake it off, and to avoid
attracting attention he moved on, but did not
speak.

Mary's eyes burned like two balls of fire as
she looked at Mr. Earnscliffe silently for a
moment or two ; but with her iron will she kept
down the fire which was raging fiercely within
her, for there must be no scene, she must be out-
wardly cool and collected so as not to lose any of
the triumph of her revenge ; and again she
spoke in measured accents. "Yes, Mr. Earnscliffe, I told you that night to dread me in the
hour when you only waited for religious rites to

make Flora Adair yours, and I promised to be near you then, so you see I have kept my word. That night you spurned me for her sake—I who had known and loved you before you ever saw her—and I swore, if it were in human power to do it, that I would tear her from you. I have done that work to-night, and *you* will *now* know what it is to have your love spurned and cast aside by your own idol for the sake of some senseless code of doctrine. And to render my revenge more full and overflowing, I have planted in her heart the thorn of distrust by making it appear that you intended to deceive her by concealing your former marriage."

"Fiend as you are," he exclaimed in a tone of suppressed passion, "you have not succeeded in that! My peerless, trusting Flora believes in me at this moment as fully as ever—— "

"How do you know that?" she interrupted eagerly.

"Because I have spoken to her since you have been trying to poison her mind against me."

Mary's coolness began to give way. Was it then possible that Flora would disappoint her of her revenge by giving up her religion rather than her lover? and she cried hotly, "And will she marry you all the same?"

Mr. Earnscliffe ground his teeth with rage.

He could not answer that question confidently. He hesitated, and in a moment all Mary's coolness came back to her. She guessed how it was: that Flora had been too confused to give any decided answer, but at the same time that he dreaded she would not marry him ; and from that instant Mary felt *sure* of her revenge. So, resuming her calm, mocking tone, she said, "Tomorrow, I suppose, you will go to her, and your 'peerless, trusting Flora' will say to you, ' I am very sorry, but my Church will not allow me to marry you,' and your love, your misery, and your reproaches will not be able to win from this passionless disciple of her Church's teaching a single concession. It is I, too, who have brought all this to bear, in order to requite you for your appreciation of the gift which I once bestowed upon you ; and my thanks are adequate, are they not, Mr. Earnscliffe ? Now take me back,—I have had all the refreshment which I wanted."

Mr. Earnscliffe did not trust himself to answer. He feared to lose all mastery over himself, for if ever a man could be tempted to forget himself, he was then. Every member trembled with the intensity of his passion as he muttered under his breath, " Demon, and worse than demon ! and yet I must allow her to go unchained."

As soon as Mary saw that they were near her mother, she let go his arm, and making him a mockingly gracious bow, she said, "Good-night, Mr. Earnscliffe, and happy dreams." He hurried downstairs, and dashing on his opera hat, which he had in his hand, he walked out into the *Place*, without ever thinking of asking for his coat, and it was between five and six in the morning when he appeared at his hotel door in full ball costume.

In the mean time Mary Elton stood for about five minutes beside Mrs. Elton without speaking, and then said abruptly, "There is Mr. Maunsell, mamma; ask him to have the carriage called, and let us go home."

Mrs. Elton had been speaking to some old acquaintances whom she had unexpectedly met a few moments before, but now she looked up at Mary to see what had caused this sudden fancy, and she felt really frightened at her appearance. There were two deep red spots on her cheeks, and her eyes glittered with a strange light. Mrs. Elton said, "Mary, you ought not to have been allowed to come to this ball; would that I had not consented to it; however you are right in wishing to go home now," and she beckoned to Mr. Maunsell to come to her, and asked him to get the carriage called.

When they stopped at their own door Mr. Maunsell got out first, then Mrs. Elton, but Mary did not move, and her mother called, "Mary are you asleep?"

No answer came, and Mrs. Elton exclaimed, "A light, for God's sake!" The servant pulled out one of the carriage lamps and held it inside, and there, with her head thrown back upon the cushions, and blood trickling from her lips, they saw Mary.

"Oh my God!" cried her poor mother, whilst Mr. Maunsell and the servant took Mary out of the carriage and carried her upstairs. Mr. Maunsell bent down his ear to catch some words which she was trying to utter, and as well as he could make out they were, "Telegraph for Lena."

CHAPTER VII.

THE great Dr. O—— was instantly sent for, telegrams to Helena and Charles were despatched, and all that human skill or care could do was done to save Mary; but while waiting for the doctor's sentence to be pronounced and Helena's arrival from Ireland, we shall turn our attention to our heroine and the coming interview with her lover.

On this fatal morning after the ball, when Flora went into the breakfast-room, where her mother and Marie were before her, the former exclaimed as she kissed her, "My child, what is the matter? You look very ill; are you so?"

"No," answered Flora, speaking hurriedly to cover her intended *équivoque*, "not now; but I certainly did suffer during the night. Neuralgia *is* dreadful torture. But where is Edward?"

"Oh, he desired us not to wait breakfast for him, as he would probably be very late, and we are going out early."

"For what?" asked Flora, listlessly.

"Oh, you *méchante* Flore!" cried Marie; "I do believe that you have forgotten the—the—*prise d'habit*—what you call it in English?—at the Sacré Cœur to-day."

"You are right; I had forgotten it. But at all events *I* cannot go: I have an appointment for this morning."

But Marie had no notion of letting her off so easily, and she said with a pout, "With whom then, Flore? You were not free to make a rendezvous for this morning when you had already promised to come with us; it would disappoint me so, and you do not wish to make pain to your Mignonne, Flore; is it not so?"

"It is impossible, Mignonne; I expect Mr. Earnscliffe," replied Flora shortly, and oh, how difficult she found it to utter that name calmly!

"*O ce Monsieur Earnscliffe!* You cede every-thing to him, Flore. But why not see him in the afternoon? Remit him until then. You can come very well if you like; can she not, Mrs. Adair?"

Flora looked at her mother so appealingly, as she would say, "Spare me, by ending this dis-cussion," that Mrs. Adair said with a smile, "Oh, Marie, you are too hard upon her. Remember who it is that you ask her to give up for the reception; and she is tired from suffering and not sleeping last night; so we will not tease her any more, but go to get ourselves ready, and leave her love-sick highness to herself and her beloved." Mrs. Adair stood up, and taking Marie by the hand, she drew her along with her, and left the room.

As the door closed on them Flora sank back in her chair with a deep sigh. How many home-thrusts had she not received in that short time! and from those who would have done anything in their power to save her from pain.

When she heard their descending steps, and the drawing up of the carriage which was to take them to the Rue de Varennes, she went tô the window and saw them drive away. Then turning back to the table, she drank off the cup of strong tea which had for so long remained untouched before her, rang to have the breakfast things taken away, and proceeded to her own room. Opening the *armoire*, she took out a box of exquisitely inlaid woods, and placed it upon the table. She raised the lid, and disclosed to view a perfectly fitted jewel case, with numerous and costly ornaments reposing in their velvet beds. But three of these were unfilled. Did she seek their occupants as her eyes wandered round the room, and rested finally on the pearl

necklace and bracelets lying on the dressing-
table, where they had lain since she took them
off last night? Yes, it was these which she
sought; but what stinging memories of that
night's awful struggle did they call up! It
almost seemed as if the struggle were going to
begin over again, as, clasping her hands together,
she cried, "It is too much! I cannot—cannot
do it!" And once more she impatiently walked
up and down the room. . . .

What! after the murmured "My God, now
teach me to do Thy will!" and the hours passed
on her knees before the crucifix, does she fall
back into the old rebellious feelings? "It is
very unheroine-like, very imperfect!" we hear
our readers exclaim. And it is quite true; but
we did not promise them a heroine even border-
ing on perfection. We know that it would be
much more according to the general style of
tale-writing to represent our heroine, after she
has made the sacrifice, as a picture of sad,
touching resignation, thinking beautiful thoughts
about the sorrow and trials which are sent to
us by an all-loving heavenly Father, receiving
them without a murmur because they come from
Him; but, alas! as we are painting from reality,
we cannot draw Flora different from what she
is—one capable of making grand sacrifices, but

unable to bear patiently the incessant pricking
of that crown of thorns which now pressed her
brows. To be really resigned, to endure without
repining, hour after hour, and day after day,
the weight of a great abiding sorrow, requires
ardent faith and sensible love of God. All this
Flora had never possessed; her faith had always
been more or less beset by struggles, and now
has come the crowning one, which may never
cease but in death. For her indeed,

> " Henceforth time is sunless,
> And day a thing that is not."

Suddenly she stood still and said, " Is this the
way in which the heroes of old sacrificed themselves to save their country? And shall I be
less brave than they were when the sacrifice
which I am called upon to make is one required by God, and made to save—although he
will not understand it *now*—him whom I love?
No, no; even though their sacrifice was far less
than mine; for they died, and were at rest,
whilst I live to suffer. But, *fiat!* " . . . She took
the necklace and bracelets and put them into
their places; her fingers seemed to cling to
them. Ah, how happy she was when she put
them on last night! and now—but she was
determined to be strong, and hastily closing the

box, she carried it into the drawing-room and seated herself on the sofa.

Reader, do you know what it is to listen for a step whose sound makes all your pulses throb; -to long for it, and yet dread it; to shudder if you think you hear it, and yet sink back with a feeling of weariness and disappointment if it comes not? If you do, we need not give any description of what Flora's feelings were as she sat in the drawing-room awaiting the arrival of Mr. Earnscliffe, for you know them by experience, and if you do not, a description of them would be useless, for words could never give you any true idea of the reality.

Her state of suspense was ended at last; the servant opened the door and announced "Monsieur Earnscliffe." She stood up, but remained leaning with one hand on the arm of the sofa, not daring to look at him. He advanced towards her, and in a constrained tone said, "Well, Flora, how are we to meet?"

"Edwin!" and she raised her eyes to his.

The look of suffering in her face put to flight his assumed coldness, and putting his arm round her waist, he kissed her forehead, drew her down on the sofa beside him, and said, "My poor darling! you look wretchedly ill; and no wonder, if you have passed as miserable a night

as I have done. Those dreadful words of yours
at the ball haunted me, and presentiments of
evil gave me no rest; but now that I am here
they do not dare to assail me as before. Now
that my Flora has had time to think calmly
over our case, I am sure she will be to me like
a good enchantress, and break all these dark
spells; will she not?"

Flora could not speak. Each word of his was
driving in the sword deeper and deeper, and she
was not deceived by his apparently cheerful
conclusion, for she knew how agitated he must
be when his "deep-toned voice faltered" as it
did now. What could she say? How was she
to begin? And the longer the silence continued,
the more difficult did it become to her to break
it. Mr. Earnscliffe, however, did that for her,
as he said suddenly, "Flora, you asked me last
night what caused my dread of Mary Elton,"—
his lips literally grew white as he named her,
and the hoarse tone of his voice made Flora
look wonderingly at him,—"and I did not answer
you; but now I think it right to do so, as it
might appear that it proceeded from fear of her
telling you about that unhappy divorce, although
in reality I could not have had any dread of that,
believing as I did that you understood it all
perfectly before you promised to be mine."

"Edwin, I did not doubt you, though appearances were so strongly against you."

"I know it, dearest; but it is better that you should be aware of what my real feelings were in regard to her. I offended her, but through no fault of mine, and in revenge she did all she could to keep me away from you; but when she saw that that was not possible, she swore, if it were in human power, to tear you from me. I had suffered so much from a woman before, that this threat of another's had a strangely powerful effect on me, and caused that morbid, and it seemed unreasonable, dread of her. I considered myself bound in honour not to tell you all this until now that she has openly interfered to separate us. But she will fail if you are only true to me, if you prove yourself to be what I have ever thought you—the first, the noblest of women, in mind as well as in heart."

She looked up at him, and her lips moved, but no words could be heard; and she shook her head as if to say, "I cannot;" then let it fall back on the cushions of the sofa.

"For God's sake, Flora, say something! I can bear this no longer. If you love me, tell——"

"If? Oh, Edwin!"

Her tone was so heart-broken, that he exclaimed, "Forgive me, Flora; but you madden me. . . . In pity speak!"

He took her hand and held it tightly in his.

"Then, Edwin," she said, with a kind of gasp, "you must try to listen to me quietly, and, above all, do not interrupt me, for I have scarcely strength to get through the miserable task which lies before me; yet it must be done. I tried to convince you in past happy days that there was to be found on earth that which you had so long sought for in vain, namely, an unerring source of truth; and its voice declares that there can be no divorce between those whom God has joined. Therefore, were I even wicked enough to be ready to barter my own soul for the intense earthly happiness of being yours, I must not do it for *your* sake; for if I did I should be only a curse to you—a curse which would prevent you from ever possessing the light of truth, that light which alone can satisfy your great mind. No, think it not, my beloved—even such unreserved love as mine could not satisfy you, unless you could look forward with undoubting hope to the continuance and perfecting of our happiness in an eternal union; then it would be bliss indeed! But as it is, my very worship of you forces me to say that we must part."

Her voice sunk almost to a whisper as she

uttered the last word, but Mr. Earnscliffe heard
it all too plainly, and for a moment he remained
silent as if stunned ; then dashing away her hand,
he stood up, and looking at her almost with scorn,
exclaimed—

"For *my* sake, indeed! You might have left
that out ; it is truly adding insult to injury. But
I have deserved this for trusting, loving again a
woman. Fool that I was to imagine that I had
found one whose mind and heart soared above
their little world of petty triumphs, of inane
occupations, and hemmed in by weak prejudices
and laid-down maxims. You were only a deeper
actress than the generality; yet, Flora"—his
voice softened almost unknown to himself—"your
acting was fearfully real ; but the first obstacle
has unmasked you." He paused for a moment,
but then burst forth again : — "Yes, you are
worthy of your sex. . . . Where is now that love
which could brave death itself for me ? It seems
that it is not strong enough to get over that
narrow-minded prejudice of your Church which
says that I am married. As for what you said
about your love causing you to act thus, and
your being a curse to me if you did not do so, by
preventing me from possessing the light of truth,
it is too nonsensical. It cannot be the voice of
truth or charity which tells you that you ought

to break, to drive to desperation, the wounded heart which you had won and promised to heal, rather than to infringe an unreasonable regulation of your Church; and this, forsooth! was the Church of which you so wished me to be a member, and of whose truth you had in some degree convinced me! But this puts the finishing stroke to my wavering belief in your 'goodness of God.' Adieu, Flora! this is your work. You found me bereft of hope, but a calm fatalist; you send me from you a blasphemer."

He turned away, and walked towards the door. Flora lay like one in a trance; those bitter, cutting words appeared to have deprived her of consciousness. But again he turned, looked back, hesitated, and hastily retracing his steps, he knelt before her, saying—

"Flora, with all the strong power of my manhood have I loved you!—do I love you! Send me not from you to despair!" and the proud man almost sobbed.

Flora started up, and, grasping his outstretched hands, she cried—

"My own beloved! in mercy recal not those dreadful spirits with which I struggled the long night through—rebellion, infidelity, and all their satellites; for, as your terrible reproaches rang in my ear, they seemed to crowd around me with renewed strength; they borrowed your words, they spoke with your voice, they looked with your eyes. How, then, resist, with all my own feelings aiding them in trying to drag me from that standard to which I must cling, or else be the cause of your ruin as well as my own? Reproach me and treat my words with scorn as much as you choose, but nevertheless it is true that it is the intensity of my love for you which, with God's grace, gives me strength to act thus; and you will feel this some day, Edwin, though I may not live to see it, for it would be too dreadful to think that such a sacrifice as mine should be made in vain. Truth must dawn upon you at last, and then you will do me justice." . . . She let go his hands, and pointing to the jewel-case, she murmured—" It is mine no longer, Edwin : when may I have it sent to you ?"

He sprang to his feet, exclaiming—

" You might have spared me that at least, Flora. Do what you like with the baubles; give them away—what you will—but I cannot have them : they would be like coals of fire burning into my heart."

He strode to the other end of the room in a state of fierce agitation, and Flora felt that she was growing very weak, that she could not bear up much longer; leaning heavily on the table upon which the casket stood, she held out her right hand, and in a faltering voice muttered—

"It must be said. . . . Edwin—good-bye!"

He seized her hand, looked into her eyes yearningly for an instant, then suddenly he caught her round the waist, clasped her to his heart, and whispered—

"*Must* I go now, Flora?"

It *was* an ordeal for her. Could she tear herself from those fond encircling arms, and raise her head from that dear resting-place on his shoulder? Her colour came and went, and his breath fanned her cheek as he bent over her to catch the longed-for leave to stay. It was the supreme moment of her long struggle, and opening her closed eyes, she looked wildly round as if to ask for help; but help there was none for her, save from God. Her lips moved, in prayer perhaps; and then she murmured—

"Oh! it is cruel, Edwin, to try me so; and yet I must resist, if I would not be a curse to you. In mercy leave me, whilst still I have sense to feel that——we must part!—Edwin, go!"

His pallor was fearful and his eyes flashed as he bent one look on the wan, suffering face lying on his shoulder; and then he pushed her from him, saying in a loud voice—

"Mary Elton was right: you are a cold, pas-

sionless disciple of a senseless code of doctrine!"
and he walked towards the door.

Flora tottered to the sofa, fell heavily upon it,
and lay there motionless; but the turning of the
door-handle roused her. She looked up with a
frightened expression; her eyes met Mr. Earnscliffe's in one long, last, passionate gaze, and the
door closed, shutting out at the same moment
from Flora her life's light and the material light
of day, for she had fainted.

CHAPTER VIII

A LITTLE after eleven o'clock, Mrs. Adair and
Marie returned from the convent, and, as the
latter opened the drawing-room door, she started
back, exclaiming " Mrs. Adair, see Flore ! "

" Good heavens ! " cried Mrs. Adair, as she
rushed over to the sofa, where Flora still lay
unconscious ; " what can have happened ! " She
guessed that this fainting fit must in some way
or other be connected with Mr. Earnscliffe, and
therefore she felt that it would be better not to
call the maid ; so she said, " Marie, run and bring
me cold water and *eau de Cologne,* but do not tell
any one of this."

Marie hastened away to get the desired restora-
tives, and when she returned Mrs. Adair bathed
Flora's temples with the cold water, and held the
eau de Cologne to her nostrils, whilst Marie rubbed
her hands to try and bring a natural heat back to
them.

When, at length, Flora opened her eyes, she

found herself in her mother's arms, and saw Marie kneeling beside her, chafing her hands. She looked at them vacantly for a moment, then with a shiver reclosed her eyes; but by degrees a slight colour came to her cheeks, and the icy cold of her hands began to yield to the warmth of returning circulation. Mrs. Adair saw that she was now really reviving, and she told Marie to take away the cold water, and leave them alone. " Now, my child," she said, as she kissed Flora, and smoothed back her tossed hair, "try to tell me what has happened."

" He called me cold, passionless; he does not believe in me any longer," murmured Flora, as if to herself.

" Flora, darling, what is it all about? Has Mr. Earnscliffe proved unworthy of you?"

Unconsciously Mrs. Adair had done the best thing in the world to rouse Flora thoroughly, by thus seeming to blame Mr. Earnscliffe. She raised her head, and for the first time looked at her mother intelligently, as she said, "No, no; but it is all over between us;" and she sank back into her mother's arms.

Mrs. Adair's heart bled for her idolised child as she clasped her to it; yet she thought that it would be better to force her to speak at once, and that she would be better afterwards, so she continued, "But what has caused this, dearest? You must endeavour to tell me collectedly all about it, as Edward must be told immediately; and if it is right that he should do so, he will apply to Mr. Earnscliffe for an explanation of his conduct, which certainly appears to me to be most strange, for of course the cause of this break rests with him."

"Mamma," cried Flora, excitedly, "do not say a word against him,—he is the soul of truth and honour. I—I am the only one in fault." She stopped for a moment, and pressing her hands nervously together, she added, "But you are right; I must try to give a collected account of it all, or you will blame him, though heaven knows he deserves it not. Oh, Edwin, Edwin!" her voice died away in a low wail, and she trembled violently all over.

Mrs. Adair threw her arms round her again, and said, "My precious child, I see that it is too much for you now. Let me take you to your room, and after you have had some hours of rest you will be able to tell me."

Flora made no objection; she seemed to be utterly indifferent as to what she was to do, and without giving her mother any answer, she let her take her to her room, and settle her as comfortably as she could on the bed. Mrs. Adair

arranged the quilt over her, and then, closing the
shutters, she said, " Now, darling, I am going to
get you some quieting drink, and when you have
taken it, you will go to sleep, and awake quite
well."

Flora shivered—the thought of that awaking
was so dreadful; but she remained silent, and
Mrs. Adair left the room. She returned, however,
after a short absence, with a strong sedative, which
she made Flora take, and then she seated herself
beside the bed.

Flora was completely worn out by want of
rest and violent agitation, so that the sedative,
aided by exhausted nature, caused her soon to
fall into a deep sleep; and when Mrs. Adair
heard her heavy regular breathing continue for
some time, she stood up softly, and stole away.
She went to Marie, who was anxiously waiting to
hear of Flora, and told her that she had fallen
asleep ; then Mrs. Adair repaired to the drawing-
room to see her son, who had just come from his
hotel.

In answer to his question of where the girls
were, and what it was that made her look so sad,
she told him as much as she knew about this
unfortunate affair of Flora's. It quite enraged
him, and he hotly declared that no matter what
Flora said, Mr. Earnscliffe must have behaved in

some very strange manner, for that he never saw a girl so desperately in love as his sister was; therefore it was evident that *she* would never have broken off the marriage unless Mr. Earnscliffe himself had forced her to do it. He would go at once to Mr. Earnscliffe, and demand a full explanation.

Mrs. Adair was endeavouring to induce him to wait until Flora could give them a tolerably clear account of what had occurred, for as yet they were completely in the dark about it all, when the servant came in, and handed Mrs. Adair a letter. It was from Mr. Earnscliffe, and commenced—

"Madam,

"I feel that it is due to myself to write you a statement of what my conduct to your daughter has been from the time that I declared my love to her. Before I obtained from her a promise that she would become my wife, I told her the history of my life, although any allusion to the past was intensely painful to me; but I was determined that she should know what the great misfortune of my life had been before she accepted me.

"I told Miss Adair accordingly that years ago I had loved a beautiful girl and won her, but no sooner had I done so than I found that I was betrayed for another, and without ever seeing her again, I hurried out of England, leaving everything in my lawyer's hands. Miss Adair treated me *then* with angelic trustfulness, and, as you are aware, consented to be mine.

"Consequently I supposed that she accepted me fully understanding that it was after my marriage that I had been betrayed, and that I had got a divorce, for I had not the slightest idea that your Church arrogated to itself the power of making laws even for those who do not belong to it. But it seems that Miss Adair misunderstood me; she imagined that it was my betrothed, and not my wife, who had been false to me, until last night, when chance revealed to her the true state of the case; and this morning she deliberately informed me that she preferred to obey one of her Church's most daring and unreasonable fiats,—which declares that there is no such thing as divorce, even outside of its jurisdiction,—rather than act according to the dictates of reason, honour, and love, by fulfilling her promise to me.

"I have written this letter of explanation in order to show that I had not, as appearances would lead one to believe, any intention of concealing my wretched marriage from Miss Adair;

this would have been base deceit; and from such a charge you will, I am sure, as Miss Adair does most fully, exonerate me. Early in life one woman betrayed me; ten years later another heartlessly sacrifices me to prejudice! Truly I owe women no gratitude!

"EDWIN EARNSCLIFFE.

"Hotel de Douvres,
 "Rue de la Paix, Paris, June 14th."

"Poor, poor Flora! God help her!" exclaimed Mrs. Adair, as she finished reading the letter, and handed it to her son, who in his turn exclaimed, after having read it, "But how was it ever allowed to go so far without your knowing that Earnscliffe had been married?"

"Edward, all retrospection is useless now," answered Mrs. Adair, sadly; "but I do not think that any one has been to blame in this unhappy case. Mrs. Elton introduced us to Mr. Earnscliffe, in Rome, as an unmarried man, with whose father and mother her family had been very intimate, but they had died many many years ago, and she had lost sight of their son— he was a baby at the time of their death—until she met him on the Continent. She spoke in high terms of his personal abilities, his social position and fortune, and of these two latter advantages we know she thinks a great deal. How could I suppose then that it

was necessary to make any further inquiries about
him? And, as he says in his letter, he gave
Flora a history of his life before he asked her to
engage herself to him, which history she told me,
but of course as she understood it, or, indeed,
misunderstood it. All this misery has been caused
by her unfortunate mistake; yet it was a most
natural one. Mr. Earnscliffe evidently did not
distinctly say that it was his *wife* who had been
false to him; and Flora, supposing everybody to
know that the Church does not recognise the
divorce law, took it for granted that he had not
been married, or else that he would not have
thought of asking her—a Catholic—to be his.
The only thing about which I was not satisfied
was as to Mr. Earnscliffe's sentiments upon religion, and I besought of Flora not to marry him
unless he would become a professed believer in
Christianity, and at all events to wait a year, and
thus let him have time to study its doctrines.
But she would listen to nothing of the kind; he
was in the true faith, she declared, because he had
such an ardent desire of the knowledge of truth.
From the first he consented to all the conditions
required by the Church. Poor child, she could
not bear to insist upon his waiting a year, and
now she is obliged to send him away for ever.
You, yourself, Edward, would scarcely have been

able to keep up, if you had seen her as I did when we came in."

"Poor Flo! when can I see her?" he said, and furtively brushed away a tear; then he added, "I see now, mother, that you are right,—no one has been to blame; but it is one of the strangest and saddest occurrences imaginable; it is really worthy of Lady Georgiana Fullerton's title, 'Too Strange not to be True.' But tell me, when will poor Flo be visible?"

"Not till the evening, at all events; it will be better for her to remain perfectly quiet all day. You will come to dinner, of course."

"Yes; and there is nothing to be done now, I suppose; there would be no object in my seeing Earnscliffe?"

"None in the world; it would only give him an opportunity of railing at religion, and, as he says, at Flora's heartless sacrifice of his love to prejudice."

"Then I may as well go away, and try to kill time as well as I can until dinner; for of course you and Marie will be occupied with poor Flo. Good-bye, then, for the present."

As soon as he was gone, Mrs. Adair sat down and wrote:—

"MY DEAR MR. EARNSCLIFFE,

"I beg to acknowledge the receipt of your letter, and to assure you that we all exonerate you perfectly from having had any intention to deceive us. Poor Flora's mistake was a most unfortunate one; but as sóon as she learned what the reality was—how she learned it I do not yet know, for she has been unable to tell me anything—she could not have acted otherwise than she has done.

"However great *your* sufferings may be, *hers* far surpass them;—she has a double weight of sorrow to bear: her own, and the greater one—that of knowing that she has inflicted pain on one whom she loves, and that he has ceased to believe in her. Her first words on being roused from the fainting fit in which I found her when I came in were, 'He called me cold, passionless; he does not believe in me any longer;' and then she relapsed into insensibility. If this is heartlessness, I leave it to you to judge.

"Adieu, and believe me to be very sincerely yours,

"CAROLINE ADAIR.

"Paris, June 14th."

Having directed her letter, and desired it to be taken immediately to the Hotel de Douvres, for

Mr. Earnscliffe, she went up to Flora's darkened room, where she found Marie watching beside the poor sleeper.

Mrs. Adair's note was handed to Mr. Earnscliffe, as he sat in his room with folded arms and his head drooping upon his breast. He seized it eagerly, tore it open, and glanced his eye over it; then crushing it up in his hand, and with his teeth firmly set together, he muttered, "Psha! let her Church, to whose senseless maxims she sacrifices me, console her! But I will show what that Church is, how its teaching is destructive of all the best qualities of the human heart and mind, since it can make such a creature as Flora Adair was act in direct contradiction to reason and love. It is too foolish to say that when a man is married *only* according to the laws of the established Church of England, that that Church has not the right to annul its own act. If Rome had had anything to do with my marriage, one could understand it; but as it is—damnation, it is unbearable!" and he stamped about the room,— then rang the bell furiously.

His servant came up with a startled look in his face, and the expression of surprise to be read there increased as his master said, "Desire my bill to be prepared, and have everything ready to start by the night train for Strasbourg."

"That's done," he exclaimed, as the servant retired. "By to-morrow I shall be in the Black Forest, and there I can stay for a day or two, and draw out the plan of my book; then if I settle myself in the neighbourhood of one of the large university towns, I shall not want for help in the way of books; and converse with the German philosophers will be pleasant and useful relaxation for me, so that in six months I may hope to have it in the publisher's hands. Now I must write letters to England, to countermand all my orders. Poor Earnscliffe Court! thou art doomed ever to be deserted! ever to be without a mistress!"

Sighing deeply, Mr. Earnscliffe opened his desk and began to write.

CHAPTER IX.

AT twelve o'clock that night—the hour when, on the previous one, they had all met in the brilliant *salle* of the Hotel de Ville—an express train was whirling Mr. Earnscliffe away from Paris, Flora Adair was walking restlessly up and down her room, and Mary Elton lay upon her deathbed.

The doctor had just left her, after having, as gently as possible, told Mrs. Elton that the last ray of hope for her daughter's recovery was gone,—she was sinking, and now it was only a question of how long she might hold out. Probably she might linger until the same time to-morrow, but it was also possible that the end might come much more quickly.

The night-lamp burned dimly, the nurse dozed in an arm-chair, and Mrs. Elton knelt in despairing grief beside her dying child, her head pressed down upon the bed-clothes, as she tried to smother the sound of her convulsive sobs, and prevent them from disturbing Mary; and she thought to

herself, " I have killed her by letting her go to
that ball. I saw that she was not fit to go, and
yet through weakness I allowed it. Mary, my
most precious child, my firstborn, do not leave
me! What can the others be to me, if you are
taken? Great God, in pity give me back this
favourite one, or let me die with her!"

Mary was indeed Mrs. Elton's " most precious
child;" she resembled her father strikingly in
appearance, as also in many points of disposition,
and far more than either Charles or Helena;
therefore was she dearer to her mother than they
were. Her husband's memory was the passion
of Mrs. Elton's existence, as he himself had been
whilst he lived; so now she felt that to lose the
child who resembled him most was like losing all
that remained to her of him, and to this was
added the torture of believing that she might
have saved her if she had only been firm about
the ball. Her agony in her utter loneliness was
piteous; her favourite child was dying, and the
other two were far away; they had been tele-
graphed for, but neither of them could possibly
have come to her as yet. Helena was expected
to arrive early in the morning, but Mrs. Elton
could make no guess as to when her son might
come. He was quartered far up in the north of
Scotland, and of course he could not start in-

stantly on receipt of the telegram, as Helena would; he must wait to get leave, and thus the time of his arrival could not be counted upon.

Mary scarcely ever spoke, save to ask, " Can Lena soon be here?" But this question she repeated almost every hour, and each time it wrung her mother's heart anew, for it showed her that Mary felt herself to be dying, and that she feared she might not live to see her sister. Mrs. Elton saw with dismay that this dread was worrying her beloved child, yet she could do nothing to relieve it; and there are few sufferings more difficult to endure than this feeling of power-lessness even to give ease to one whom we love, although we must yield them up to the grave in a few short hours.

Through the whole of that lone night-watch Mrs. Elton remained on her knees beside the bed. Several times the nurse had tried to induce her to sit down, but she never answered, or appeared even to hear her; she seemed insensible to every-thing except the dying girl, but to her slightest movement, or barely audible words, she was keenly alive.

At last, about five in the morning, a carriage was heard to stop at the door. Mary quivered all over, and murmured, " Mamma, there is Lena; go to her and tell her that she must not be

frightened when she sees me. Poor Lena, it is
too bad to ask her to come almost from her
honeymoon to see me thus; and she has never
looked upon approaching death before. And you,
mamma, you must not grieve so wildly for me: I
heard your sobs and passionate prayers all through
the long night, but I did not dare to speak to
you, I was so afraid of exhausting my strength
before Lena came. Mamma, she is far more
worthy of your affection than I have been,—give
it all to her, and she will repay you well. Go to
her now."

"I cannot," murmured Mrs. Elton. "Nurse,
go and receive Mrs. Caulfield, and beg of her to
wait for a few moments in the drawing-room;"
and, with an irrepressible sob, she added, as she
clasped Mary's hand in hers, "My own child,
take me with you to your father! Life without
him and you will be too awful!"

"Shall I ever see him?" whispered Mary
fearfully. "But it is cruel to treat Lena thus.
Mamma, go to her for my sake, and let me see
her as soon as possible, and then you must go
and rest for a few hours,—I insist upon it," she
said with a faint smile; "and you know you
cannot disobey me, as it will be the last time."

Mrs. Elton turned away with a choking sensation in her throat, and left the room.

From the time that Mary had been carried from the carriage to her bed she felt that she had risked the last chance for her life, and lost it in order to gratify her revenge and gloat over the sight of her rival's misery; but even so she did not then regret it, for her triumph had been so full and complete, and every other thought was for the moment absorbed in the wish to see her sister; her affection for her being, as we have said before, the one pure feeling which not even the terrible passion of revenge could sully. But during the twenty-eight or thirty hours that she had lain on her dying bed she had been haunted by grim phantoms of terror regarding the unknown world to which she was going so fast, and she began to feel that the success of her revenge was far less sweet to think of than she had expected; now, however, Helena's coming brought up vividly before her the remembrance of that miserable night at Naples, and once more a flush of fierce satisfaction covered her face, as she muttered, "Well, at least I paid him off to the last farthing!" As these words passed her lips the door opened, and Helena entered, with the tears streaming from her eyes.

"Darling Lena!" exclaimed Mary, but without attempting to sit up, for the doctor had warned her that to do so would surely bring on a recurrence of the hemorrhage—"how good you were to come so quickly."

Helena threw herself on the bed beside Mary, and kissed her again and again, but she could not speak; and as Mary tried to soothe her, her tears only flowed the faster, until at last the former said in a broken voice, "Lena, think how you are trying me, and I have so little strength left to talk to you, or even to listen to you. I think I hear the nurse coming. Go and tell her not to come until you call her, and I begged mamma to lie down and rest for a little; so once more, Lena, you and I can have a *tête-à-tête* chat, as in days of old."

Helena silently rose, and did as Mary desired her; then returning, she seated herself beside the bed, and took her sister's cold hand in hers and began to rub it, saying, "How cold your hands are, sister!—let me warm them for you."

"They will never be warm again, Lena," answered Mary, with a sort of smile; "but never mind that now, tell me about yourself. Are you as happy as you expected to be?"

"Oh, Mary," rejoined Helena, trying to suppress her tears, "until I received that miserable telegram my happiness was unalloyed, and I only longed for the time when I could get you to come and stay with me, that you might have the pleasure of seeing what your kindness and affection had done for me; for had you not been all that you were to me, I should never have had the happiness of being Harry's. Mary, you must live to see your own work."

"Lena, how can you talk so! Has not mamma told you that by this time to-morrow I shall no longer be with you?"

"Yes," sobbed Helena; "but while there is life there is hope—and I *will* hope."

"You *must* not, Lena, for there is none; this is the second since——" a spasm caught her breath, but she went on, although her voice was evidently getting weak—"since that evening when you found me half fainting by the stone bench."

"Mary," cried Helena, almost angrily, "you have treated me shamefully in not letting me be told that you had an attack of this kind on the night of my wedding; and I saw by mamma that she blames me bitterly for having left you; she thinks that my doing so increased, even though it did not cause, your illness; and in justice to me, Mary, you ought to have written to me. I could have been with you all these weeks past since Harriet's marriage, and I might have saved you; being in your confidence, I could in

some degree have prevented you from brooding
over the past until it has killed you. Why have
you kept me away from you, sister? But tell me
what is all this about the ball, and Mr. Earnscliffe, and Flora Adair? I could not understand
anything from mamma's account of it."

"You remember the first time in Rome that
you spoke of those two names together,—I said
then that I would rather see him dead than
loving and beloved by her; then in Naples he
spurned my love for her sake, and I swore to be
revenged; and I have been!"

"Mary, for God's sake stop!" interrupted
Helena, with an expression of horror; "it is too
awful to hear the dying speak of revenge!"

But Mary resumed with increasing vehemence,
"By chance I heard that he had been married,
and that his divorced wife was living. I knew
then that *she* could not marry him, and at the
same time I was certain that *he* did not know
enough of Catholics to be aware that this would
be a barrier, so in all probability he had not told
her; therefore I could easily make it appear that
he had intended to deceive her, and thus torture
her doubly: and through my instrumentality,
too, he should feel the bitter agony of having his
love rejected by the being whom he loved. Lena,

I carried it all out at the ball, and I saw them both writhe under my blows! Ay, I paid *him* off fully for that night in Naples! Ah!——"

She half rose from her recumbent posture, and then fell back heavily. Helena caught her in her arms and screamed, "Nurse!"

The nurse was fortunately in the adjoining room, and she ran to Helena's assistance at once. She saw that her patient had only a passing faintness; and under her experienced treatment Mary soon rallied. Helena then asked her to leave them alone again, and she did so, but gravely cautioned Helena not to allow her sister to excite herself, as any violent agitation might be instantly fatal. Helena promised to do her best to prevent it, and the nurse left them.

For a full hour more the sisters' conference lasted, and then Helena went into the next room, murmuring, through her tears, "Nurse, desire a clergyman to be sent for; and wait: I must write a note, which can be left at its destination as the messenger goes to the clergyman."

Helena burst out crying afresh as she opened Mary's desk and tried to write; at last she succeeded in scribbling these few lines:—

" My dear Flora,

" Poor dearest Mary we fear is dying. She would like to see you; so I hope you will come to us as soon as you can.

" Yours affectionately,

" Helena Caulfield.

" Friday Morning."

As she gave the note to the nurse, Mrs. Elton came into the room, and Helena told her that Mary wished to see a clergyman, and also Flora Adair, and that the nurse had just gone to desire them to be sent for. Mrs. Elton passed on silently into Mary's room, and it was only the nervous quivering of her lips which told that she understood what had been said to her.

Helena had hard work to make Mary consent to receive a clergyman, and to see Flora Adair, in order to undo as far as she could the suffering which she had inflicted on her by calumniating Mr. Earnscliffe, and now she began to feel completely exhausted from fatigue and grief as she lay back in the chair after writing the note. But she was roused by Mrs. Elton, who lightly touched her shoulder, and said, like a person speaking in a dream, " Mary says that you must go and take some rest, and they will bring you breakfast."

She rang the bell, and her own maid answered it, to whom she said, "Take Miss Helena to my room, and get her tea—breakfast—you know what to do." Then Mrs. Elton turned away and went back to Mary.

Helena followed the maid into Mrs. Elton's room, and gladly lay down upon the bed, as she said, "Margaret"—the maid was an old acquaintance of hers—"if my husband comes—he went to an hotel to be out of the way at first—show him in here, and also Miss Adair; of course you will tell me at once if Miss Elton should get worse."

"Yes, miss—I beg your pardon—ma'am; and now I will go and get you some breakfast."

"It will be useless to bring me anything but a cup of tea, Margaret."

After Helena had taken the tea she fell asleep, and slept for about an hour, when she was awaked by a kiss, and the sound of somebody saying, "Poor Cricket, how unlike itself it looks, doesn't it, Miss Adair?"

As she opened her eyes, and saw her husband and Flora standing beside her, she exclaimed, "Harry, I am so glad that you have come, and Flora too; but——" She covered up her face in her hands, and the tears trickled through her closed fingers.

Margaret now came in, and said, "Mrs. Caulfield, Miss Elton has asked for you."

"Say that I will be with her in a moment," answered Helena, springing off the bed, and hastening after Margaret, as she said to Mr. Caulfield and Flora, "Wait here for me."

She was only a few moments absent, and entering with her handkerchief pressed to her eyes, she took Flora's hand and led her in to Mary, over whose countenance the livid colour of death was fast spreading.

Flora felt awe-stricken as she thought that not six-and-thirty hours had passed since she saw her in the ball-room, and silently she went over and knelt down beside the bed, as Mary said in a hollow voice, "Flora Adair, can you forgive me?"

"It was right that I should know it, Mary."

"Yes, that I understand; but can you forgive me for having tried to lower you in his opinion by falsehood, and every means in my power, and finally for insinuating to you that he was deceiving you by not telling you of his marriage, although he knew that you could not be his wife in the sight of your Church if that were known?"

Mary paused, and Flora, shuddering, said, "It was very cruel, the bare suspicion of it tortured me; but I did not believe it, or it would have driven me mad. But, Mary, what had I ever done to you that you should have thus sought to harm me?"

"You gained the love of the man whom I loved with an overwhelming love, and for you he rejected me. . . . Was this no cause to hate you? Revenge became the object of my life, and I had it,—I saw *him* suffer that night at the ball even as he had made me suffer; but that longed-for revenge has turned into bitterness, instead of sweetness, and my gentle sister there has won me to better thoughts, and induced me to send for you to ask your forgiveness, and to tell you distinctly what *I* knew all along, that *he* did not know the Catholic rules about divorce. So again I ask your forgiveness."

"You have it, Mary; although God knows you have made us both suffer doubly!" Flora rose and kissed her forehead, but she almost started at its cold, clammy touch, and Mary murmured, "Lena, it has been growing dark to me for a long time, but now it is nearly night, so call mamma and your husband; I must say good-bye to him,—I have not seen him since your wedding "—Lena sobbed violently—" and the clergyman, he may come too if you like; he is with mamma. But he cannot throw light upon the darkness into which I am entering. O God!" and Mary moaned.

That moan was heard in the next room, where her mother, her brother-in-law, and the clergyman were waiting to be called; and they stood up and went into the sick room.

Surely we may draw a curtain over these last awful moments. Poor Mary! . . . *her* dying words might have been similar to those of the great world poet—"Light, light, more light!"

Half an hour later Mrs. Elton was carried in a state of utter unconsciousness from the room of her dead child, whilst Helena sobbed away her grief in her husband's arms, and Flora Adair drove home more saddened even than when she left it some two hours before.

CHAPTER X

THAT evening Charles Elton arrived in Paris to find his sister dead, and his mother stretched on her bed like a person in a trance, with her eyes wide open, but apparently unconscious of every-thing that was going on around her. She did not even speak or move when he went into the room and kissed her. Some hours later, when he and Helena were speaking in whispers about the preparations for the funeral, she, how-ever, started up suddenly, and said, " She must be taken to England,—we will go with her and see her laid beside her father. Charles, you will arrange all this." Then slowly and deliber-ately she left the room and went into Mary's, where she remained day and night in spite of all remonstrance, until the coffin was screwed down and carried away for transportation to England. She gazed after it with tearless eyes as she stood leaning against the bed from which it had been taken, but the despair of her look

and attitude was such that it awed Helena, who
was sobbing passionately, into silence, and rising
from her knees she went and wound her arms
round her mother, and tried by her caresses to
soften the bitterness of her grief, but Mrs. Elton
seemed to shrink from her, and after a few
minutes she said, coldly, " When do we start ? "

" At six this evening," murmured Helena;
" the packet leaves Havre for Southampton at
twelve to-night."

Mrs. Elton then disengaged herself from
Helena, and going into her own room she
remained there alone with her sorrow, for Helena
did not venture to follow her. This unnatural
composure and coldness in their mother rendered
the journey to England even more sad and silent
to Helena and Charles than it must have been
under any circumstances, and had it not been for
Harry Caulfield's comparative cheerfulness and
activity of mind it would have been almost
unbearable.

The Eltons had a beautiful place in the neighbourhood of Southampton, and in the pretty
retired cemetery close by, Mary was, according to
Mrs. Elton's wishes, to be laid beside her father.
On the evening of the funeral, when the sun's
last rays had faded into twilight, and all nature
seemed settling into repose, Mrs. Elton contrived

to steal out unperceived to visit the joint tomb of her beloved husband and child. At the sight of it, and the thought of the two idols of her heart lying there, side by side, but insensible and unknown to each other, her icy composure gave way, and with a heart-broken cry she cast herself on the dewy ground which covered them. Then the long-suppressed tears burst forth in torrents, and an hour afterwards her two remaining children, after seeking her in vain all through the house, found her still crouched over the grave, weeping bitterly. It was a relief to them to see her cry, for now that her grief had a natural vent in tears they hoped that it would gradually become less overwhelming. They silently knelt down beside her, and their tears flowed too over a father and sister's grave. Then gently they raised their mother from the ground and induced her to return home with them, but scarcely had she entered the house when she was seized with a violent fit of shivering. They got her to bed as quickly as possible, and made her take hot drinks, but the shivering fits returned at intervals, and the next morning they sent for a doctor. He at once pronounced her illness to be fever, and for three weeks life and death seemed to be hanging in equal balance; but life, for the present at least, outweighed death, and Mrs. Elton slowly began

to amend. Charles and Helena had been devoted
in their attendance upon her during those weary
one-and-twenty days, and now, as she daily
regained a little strength, she used silently to
clasp their hands in hers, whilst her countenance
showed how much she felt their affectionate soli-
citude about her. And when at last she was able
to go about again, she was quite a changed person;
all the seeming coldness and self-reliance of her
character had vanished, and she appeared to lean
on Helena's affection.

Charles was obliged to rejoin his regiment, so
the Caulfields persuaded her to accompany them
to Ireland, and spend the remainder of the year
with them, promising at the same time that they
would return to England with her in the spring.
And they did so, but, as it turned out, only to
follow Mrs. Elton to her last home, for before
spring's budding foliage had ripened into the
maturity of summer, her weary spirit was set at
rest, and she was laid beside the two whom she
had so loved in life.

Here ends our record of the Elton family, and
the story returns to the Adairs.

Mr. Adair went back to Ireland, regretting for
his own sake as well as his sister's that fruitless
visit to Paris; and, as soon as the hapless 21st was
past, the remainder of the party went down to the

south of France, to the de St. Severans, where they were received indeed with open arms.

Monsieur de St. Severan was a favourable specimen of a Frenchman of the old school, full of courtesy and compliment to ladies, but so delicately was the latter insinuated and interwoven in manner and speech that it never appeared fulsome or offensive. In appearance he was somewhat above the middle height, and very thin; his eyes were dark brown and his features marked and pointed; his countenance in repose was very grave, but his smile was like a sunbeam bursting through the clouds on a dull grey afternoon, it was so bright and genial. With such a smile did he welcome and fold Marie in his arms, as he murmured, "*Ma chère enfant, enfin je te revois.*"

Madame de St. Severan was quite different. She was a short, plump, merry-looking Irishwoman, with frank, at times somewhat abrupt, cordial manners. She had evidently been pretty in her style, and even still retained a fair share of comeliness. She too received Marie most affectionately, and warmly joined in her husband's elaborate expression of thanks to Mrs. Adair for thus conducting their adopted child to their very arms.

It may be remembered that Flora did not wish the de St. Severans to be told of her intended

marriage until it was on the eve of taking place,
so now they knew nothing of her great sorrow.
This was principally the reason why Mrs. Adair
had induced her to consent to their accompanying
Marie to the chateau, as with the de St. Severans
she knew there would be a complete change of
scene and association for her; there could be no
allusions to the past, no recollections of bygone
happy hours excited. Besides, being with complete strangers, she would be obliged to exert
herself more or less, and thus Mrs. Adair hoped
she would be roused from that state of sad silent
abstraction in which she now lived. For the
first week the plan seemed to have succeeded.
Flora appeared to interest herself in everything,
and quite won Monsieur de St. Severan's admiration; like most foreigners, he cared even more
for agreeability than for beauty; but at the end
of that week she was seized with a violent attack
of neuralgia in the head; nothing seemed to give
her any ease, and for four days the pain continued
with almost maddening intensity; then, however,
it began gradually to subside, and at length it
ceased altogether; but almost her first words after
she got ease were, " Mamma, take me home,—this
is too much for me."

Mrs. Adair now saw what it was, and that it
was better even to allow her to brood over her

grief than to force her to make the exertion of
mixing in society; and so, in spite of all the de
St. Severans' warm entreaties for a longer visit,
they left the chateau after about a fortnight's
stay, and journeyed slowly towards Ireland. If
Flora had any wish, save not to be obliged to see
people, it was to be near her friend Mina Blake;
yet it scarcely amounted to a wish; even friendly
conversation and sympathy could give her but
little pleasure, for now she felt how true was the
saying, " *Mieux se taire que de parler faiblement
de ce que l'on éprouve fortement,*" and to speak of
anything but that one subject was almost impossible to her, for in it was her whole mind
absorbed. She had sent her lover from her
rather than forswear the cause of truth, but to
banish him from her thoughts and heart she did
not attempt; indeed it would have been difficult
to convince her that there was anything wrong
in thus clinging to the memory of her short span
of happiness. Nevertheless she wished much to
get home and have some settled occupation, to try
to while away the weary, weary time.

Marie was, as she herself said, " *desolée* " at
being separated from " Flore," and her parting
whisper was, " When you write you will sometimes tell me news of him, Flore,—except through
you, I shall never even hear his name again."

Flora, of course, promised to do so, and after the first burst of irrepressible tears which followed the Adairs' departure, Marie began to feel that indulging such grief for her friends might hurt her adopted parents, who lavished so much affection upon her, so for their sakes she tried with all her usual amiability to appear cheerful. The task was not an easy one, particularly at first; but by degrees it became less difficult as she lost all remnant of shyness with Monsieur de St. Severan, and treated him as a petted daughter would a doating father. Madame de St. Severan was very kind and indulgent to her; yet Marie never felt towards her as she did to her "*cher père.*" Of companionship of her own age she had not much, and what she had did not give her much pleasure. There were a few families in the neighbourhood where there were young ladies, but, unlike herself, they were prim and apparently retiring, so that when Marie did meet them it only made her think how different they were from "Flore." Therefore, notwithstanding all her praiseworthy exertions, and partly successful ones, to be cheerful and contented, it was a relief to her when October came, and they set out for Paris, where she had the prospect of a gay winter before her, and much more variety of every kind than she could have in the country;

besides, almost unacknowledged to herself did she
cherish an expectation of meeting Mr. Barkley
there.   She had not forgotten one pleasant
evening's walk on the banks of the golden Arno,
when he said something about intending to go to
Paris during the ensuing winter, and asked
casually what was Monsieur de St. Severan's
address there.   She remembered, too, that he
wrote down the address as soon as she told it to
him, so it was a possibility that he might come
and see them, and beyond that she did not
venture to let her thoughts wander.

Christmas passed, however, and no Mr. Barkley
appeared, but early in January there came a
letter from Flora, saying, she heard that he and
his father were going immediately to Paris to
meet, it was said, their friends the Molyneuxes,
who were spending the winter there for the
advantage of their only daughter, whom it was
supposed Lord Barkley wanted his son to marry.
Poor Marie! the realisation of her hope that
Edmund Barkley would come to Paris now promised to bring her pain rather than pleasure.
She knew the Molyneuxes well,—they were most
intimate with the de St. Severans.   The young
lady was to have an enormous fortune, and she
was undoubtedly very handsome, but hers was
indeed—

"A beauty for ever unchangingly bright,
  Like the long, sunny lapse of a summer day's light,
  Shining on, shining on, by no shadow made tender."

There were none of the lovely lights and shades of Autumn. She was statuesque in appearance, and her manner was quite in keeping with her countenance, ever formal, cold, and inanimate. And this was the one for whom Mr. Barkley was expected to give up his bright, playful Marie, whose soft prettiness

" Now melting in mist, now breaking in gleams,"

varied with every passing feeling.

How true it is that we are always prone to think that our misfortune, whatever it might be, would be easier to bear if it were but different in this or that particular! So now Marie thought if Edith Molyneux were another sort of person, one, in short, whom Mr. Barkley could have loved and been happy with, that she would not have found it so difficult to give him up to her; but as it was it seemed doubly hard to bear. Then too she was obliged to try and hide it all away in the recesses of her own heart, for, except Flora, no one knew anything of her unhappy love,—she had not had courage to make a confidant of Monsieur de St. Severan, although he sometimes questioned her anxiously as to what made her at times, when she thought herself unobserved, look so sad and thoughtful; and more than once she was on the point of telling him the whole history ; but she was always stopped by the fear of his blaming Mr. Barkley and becoming prejudiced against him.

Some few nights after she had received Flora's letter, she sat in company with Monsieur de St. Severan and the Molyneuxes, in an opera box, listening with glowing cheeks and glistening eyes to Mario's thrilling tones as they rang forth the "*Non ti scordar di me*" of "*A che la morte;*" and so absorbed was she that she did not know that the box door had opened, and two gentlemen had entered unperceived by her, until a low murmur of voices from behind disturbed her enjoyment of the music, and looking round impatiently, her eyes met Mr. Barkley's. It was all she could do to repress the cry of joy which trembled on her lips as she gave him her hand. He pressed it silently, but his lips seemed to form and follow the passionate words which Mario now sang, " *Sconto col sangue mio l'amor che posi in te.*" The last eight months, Miss Molyneux, everything, did Marie forget in that moment, save that her lover was with her, and apparently true, and the tears which stole down her cheeks, as the devoted but hapless Leonora expired in the arms of her " true love," were mingled tears of real pleasure and fictitious sorrow. But as the curtain fell and the dewy mist cleared away from before her eyes, she saw a sight which dashed all her bright joy and recalled to her her real position.

Standing behind Miss Molyneux's chair, and leaning over it with marked attention, was an old gentleman bearing a strong resemblance to Mr. Barkley. Marie, of course, knew that this must be his father even before Mr. Molyneux said—

"Ah, Mademoiselle Marie! I must introduce you to my friend, Lord Barkley, though I see that you are already acquainted with his son."

Marie thought she perceived his lordship frown as he bowed to her, and said with a chilling smile—

"I have heard of Mademoiselle Arbi from my daughter, Mrs. Penton, who met her travelling in Italy last year with some acquaintances of ours." And turning to Colonel de St. Severan, to whom he had been already introduced, he added more graciously—"Her kind protector, Colonel de St. Severan's name is one too noted to be unknown to any one who has been much in France."

Colonel de St. Severan seemed to be pleased at this, and said he hoped to have the "*honneur*" of receiving his lordship at his hotel. The two old gentlemen then fell into a conversation upon the African wars, and Edmund, in obedience to a glance from his father, turned to Miss Molyneux, and tried to *make* her talk; whilst Marie leaned over the box's parapet, and feigned to be much occupied with the light afterpiece which followed the opera; yet had she been suddenly asked what it was about, she could no more have told than she could tell what was going on in Algiers at that moment.

Mr. Barkley did not, however, continue his efforts at " doing the agreeable " to Miss Molyneux very long, and Marie's painful thoughts were broken in upon by his bending over her chair, and asking in a low tone—

" Has Miss Arbi, then, forgotten Italy and the friends whom she met there, and whom, in those days, she seemed to honour with her regard, for she has not once bid me welcome to Paris? "

Marie looked up at him, and in her large truthful eyes might be read an expression of gentle but sorrowful reproach, as she said, " One forgets not always that which one ought to forget; also I have not forgotten Italy, and if I have not *said*, be welcome, I felt it."

" Ah! Mademoiselle, if you only knew how the memory of Italy has haunted me, you would not be so chary of your acknowledgment that you too

had not forgotten it. I may have the happiness
of seeing you here, may I not?"

"I have heard my dear father ask Lord
Barkley to come to see us, and perhaps you will
come with *Monsieur votre père.*"

"Can *you* doubt it?"

"But you will be very occupied with your
friends the Molyneuxes. You are come to Paris
to meet them, are you not?" and involuntarily
she glanced at Miss Molyneux.

"Marie!" he whispered,—then looking towards
the stage, as if he were alluding to the opera
which they had just seen, he repeated aloud, "The
words, '*Sconto col sangue mio l'amor che posi
in te,*' harmonise so well with the air.".

"Yes, '*A che la morte,*' it is a melody so
sweet," she answered, endeavouring to follow his
example in seeming to talk of the music; but
a bright flush spread itself over her face as she
now heard him utter the words which before she
only imagined she saw his lips silently form.

If such moments could only be lasting! But—

"The brightest still the fleetest."

There was a general movement in the house;
the performance was over and the audience all
prepared to depart. Lord Barkley came forward
and offered his arm to Marie, saying, "You

must allow an old man, Mademoiselle, to have the pleasure of escorting you to your carriage, and so give him an opportunity of becoming somewhat better acquainted with you, and Edmund will no doubt take good care of my old friend Molyneux's fair daughter."

"Edmund" did *not* look delighted with this arrangement, but there was no help for it now; so with as good a grace as he could command in the midst of his annoyance, he obeyed the parental injunction, and took Miss Molyneux down.

Meanwhile, Marie timidly laid her hand on Lord Barkley's arm, as she tried to get a sidelong glimpse at his face, to see if he looked very sternly at her, and she felt a little reassured on finding that his countenance was quite the contrary of stern. His age might have been about sixty, and his hair and moustache were quite white. He had full ruddy cheeks, rather small blue eyes, full lips, and a thick nose, not quite guiltless of a suspicious vermilion tint. The expression of his face was altogether more that of a good-natured, jolly old *bon vivant*, than of a severe, unrelenting parent; and Marie would not have been dissatisfied with the impression which she made on him, had she known that as he handed her into the carriage he said to himself,

" By Jove! I can't find fault with Edmund's taste
in preferring this pretty, coy little creature, to
that stiff, Juno-like beauty. If I were a young
man myself, I should be sure to fall in love with
the little one! Therefore, I am doubly sorry to
be obliged to thwart the poor fellow; but I must
do it for the sake of the family as well as his
own. He would be a poor man all his life if I
let him marry without a large fortune."

As the father and son walked home, the former
said, " Edmund, my boy, I have just a few words
to say to you about Miss Arbi. I think her very
charming."

" So I perceived, sir," interposed Edmund,
drily; " you lingered over the putting-on of her
cloak with the courtly grace of a Leicester."

" Eh, boy, jealous are you?" replied the old
man, with a chuckle; " but, seriously, I think her
—as I have said—charming, and I should be
delighted to see her your wife, if you could afford
to marry without a good many thousands; therefore take my advice—don't go too far with her;
that peppery old colonel mightn't like it. And I
tell you again, I must do all I can not to allow
you to ruin yourself by making an imprudent
marriage; but if you will do it, I'll save the
property, at least, by leaving it to Marie's second
boy."

"This is the old story over again, sir," retorted his son, impatiently, "and I accompanied you to Paris on the express condition that you would endeavour to learn what fortune Monsieur de St. Severan will give Miss Arbi, and that you would then think about whether you would grant me your consent or not. The moment I meet her, however, you begin to lecture me about being prudent and keeping clear of her. If this was to be the way of it, it would have been better for us to have remained at home. Now, of course, I understand why you were so anxious that we should come to Paris: it was to try and entangle me with that block of ice, Miss Molyneux; but I'll not have her, father."

"Very well, just as you like, my dear boy, but you certainly might do worse. She is very rich, very beautiful—as you must admit—and I have reason to know that her family would be very willing to receive you as a suitor for her hand. But, all the same, I'll keep my promise about Miss Arbi, and if I can avoid it I'll throw no obstacle in the way. However, to be candid with you, Edmund, I feel certain that she can't have nearly enough for you. Why, ten thousand pounds would be an immense fortune for a foreigner to have, and that would be of no earthly use to you. So, for your own sake and hers, don't be too much with her—don't, at all events, make her remarkable before her friends, the Molyneuxes."

"How very anxious you are about her, sir; but leave that to me,—I'll take care not to make her remarkable. Good-night, sir," he added abruptly, as they got into the hotel; and he hastily took a candle and walked off in high dudgeon to his room.

Again Mr. Barkley was acting a cowardly, ungenerous part towards Marie in making these professions of love, although he should have known in his heart that his father would not be satisfied with anything that Colonel de St. Severan could give her, and that he himself had not the courage to marry her in spite of that, and so risk the loss of his hereditary estate, which, as we have just heard, his father threatened to leave away from him if he married any one whose fortune was not sufficient to clear it. Had he even been wholly dependent upon this, there might have been some excuse for him, but, on the contrary, he was actually in possession of a small property of about five hundred a year, which had been left to him by an uncle; but this seemed absolute penury to the luxurious heir of at least as many thousands per annum. He persuaded himself, however, that on the strength of his father's approbation of Marie personally, and his promise to inquire what her fortune might be, he was authorised in devoting himself to please her.

Accordingly, he sought her society in every possible way; and through the Molyneuxes, with whom his father was always pleased to see him, he contrived to get up riding parties, parties to operas, concerts, balls, &c. One day during a ride in the Bois de Boulogne, the party consisting of himself, Marie, Mr. and Miss Molyneux, the latter's horse became restive in the crowd, and Mr. Barkley suggested that they should get into some of the less-frequented alleys, where the animal would probably go quite quietly; he undertook to lead the way with Marie, whilst Mr. Molyneux and his daughter followed. Here on the first favourable occasion he renewed his protestations of undying love to Marie, and won timid avowals of the same nature from her. He told her—with a slight colouring it is true—of his father's promise, and how he only lived in the hope of being soon able to ask Colonel de St. Severan for her hand.

Marie listened in delight, and thought to herself—" Flore did not do him justice. How little he really cares about money ; for notwithstanding Miss Molyneux's wealth, and beauty too, he is true to me." Then she said aloud in her low, sweet voice, " How happy you have rendered

me! But I must tell my dear father all this, or
I would feel that I deceived him."

"Marie, for my sake you must not speak to
him yet. Only have a little patience. If you
tell Colonel de St. Severan now, he will be sure to
apply to my father at once in true French style,
and then adieu to all my hopes. My father, taken
thus suddenly, and before I have time to gain
him over to all I wish, would peremptorily refuse
his consent."

"No, no. I would pray my dear father for
love of me to say nothing of it to anybody; but
he would be wounded if I hide from him the
truth. I *must* tell him, Edmund!"

Mr. Barkley drew himself up haughtily as he
replied—

"Pray do not suppose that I wish to bind you
to secresy further than that I know if you speak
to Colonel de St. Severan now there will be an
end to everything between you and me; but if
you are *satisfied* that it should be so, I have no
more to say. Miss Arbi is, of course, perfectly at
liberty to act as she thinks right; only it would
have been more candid had she told me from the
beginning that she was not so deeply interested
in the case as I flattered myself."

A vivid colour rushed up to Marie's face,
mounting to her very temples, and for an instant

her eyes flashed with indignation as she looked full at him ; but it was only for a moment : the next, her bright eyes became suffused in tears, and without a word she turned away her head.

Marie had never appeared so lovely to Mr. Barkley as now. That sudden flash of anger, as he accused her of want of candour towards himself, which darted across her countenance, then faded into an expression of such deep sadness, seemed to him the prettiest and most touching thing he had ever seen, and he exclaimed, eagerly—

"Forgive me, my sweet Marie! How could I be so heartless as to say anything which could pain you? I know that you are all truth and candour ; but the fact is, I scarcely know what I say. I am driven half wild between love of you and fear of not being able to marry you ; and if you would not destroy all my hopes of ever having that happiness, do not tell Colonel de St. Severan for a few days longer, at all events. I know well that nothing you or any one else could say to him would prevent him from speaking to my father. Marie, here come the others! Will you promise me to be silent, at least until I can speak to you again on the subject?"

There was no time to expostulate any farther, and, half frightened at the suppressed vehemence of his voice, she murmured—"Yes."

He looked his thanks as the others came alongside of them, and for the remainder of the ride he attached himself to Miss Molyneux's side.

Marie went home looking so pale and tired, that Colonel de St. Severan, with fond anxiety, blamed himself for allowing her to take such long rides. He little knew that it was not fatigue, but remorse for the promise which she had given to deceive him—as it seemed to her—even for a time, that made her look so pale, and every mark of affection which he bestowed upon her increased this feeling.

Things went on in the same state for about ten days. Mr. Barkley, Marie thought, appeared to avoid any opportunity of speaking to her privately, although his manner to her, whenever he did meet her, was expressive of the utmost devotion; but her self-reproach for her conduct to her kind adopted father increased daily, and one afternoon, when she thought every one was out, she gave free vent to her tears as she lay on the sofa in the drawing-room, murmuring every now and then—

"Edmund, Edmund! why did you wring from me that unfortunate promise? My dear father, how much less unhappy I should be if I could tell you everything! It is terrible to feel that I am playing false to the one if I keep my word, and to the other if I break it! Terrible to be divided between my lover and my father! *Oh, mon père!*"

"*Ma chère enfant!*" said a voice close to her, and she was clasped in Colonel de St. Severan's arms.

He had heard all : so now there could be no further secresy, and in answer to her cry on seeing him, "What have I done? Edmund will say that I have broken my word to him!" he said—

"*I* am the witness that you have kept it but too well, until it made you almost ill. Had Providence not sent me home unexpectedly to-day, I should still have been in ignorance, and you would have been suffering."

When he had petted her into something like composure, he gently but firmly insisted upon hearing the whole history, assuring her that it was better he should know all than be left to form his own conjectures. She felt that he was right, and so she told him everything from the beginning in Florence, and tried to make Mr. Barkley's conduct appear in as favourable a light as possible; but Colonel de St. Severan's countenance grew darker and darker as she proceeded, till she came to the account of how Mr. Barkley made her promise to be silent, in spite of all her entreaties to be allowed to tell him; then his indignation burst forth, and he denounced him as a *vaurien—un homme déshonorable.* But Marie now fell into such a state of agitation that it almost frightened him, and so passionately did she plead for "Edmund," that Colonel de St. Severan said at last—

"In order to save you from grief, *ma fille chérie,* I will give this gentleman a chance. I know from Molyneux that he has, independent of his father, an annual rent of from twelve to fifteen thousand francs, and I will give you a *dot* of three hundred thousand francs; therefore, if he really loves you, he can marry you without any assistance from his father."

Marie's gratitude knew no bounds. Poor confiding child, she never for a moment doubted her lover, and wild with joy she ran up to her room to wash away the traces of tears before Madame de St. Severan should come in.

The next day was their reception day, and among other visitors came Mr. Barkley. He saw that Mary looked flushed and excited, but gayer than he had ever seen her since the old days in Florence; and her gaiety jarred upon him, as he himself was in wretched spirits, his father having just told him finally that he must either give up all idea of marrying Miss Arbi, or of ever possessing Barkley Castle. *Neither* could he resolve to give up, and his object in paying that visit to the de St. Severans was to hear if they would be at the ambassador's ball that night, when he intended to have another conversation with Marie. Thus, his vexation was considerably increased on being told that they had sent an apology. Marie having looked so ill for the last few days, they were determined not to allow her to undergo any new fatigue.

He stood up to go away, feeling angry with the de St. Severans for not going to the ball, and with Marie for appearing gay when he was so miserable. Colonel de St. Severan left the room with him, and as soon as the drawing-room door was closed, he requested Mr. Barkley to grant him a few minutes' conversation in his study.

"She has betrayed me!" he thought, as he followed Colonel de St. Severan into the study.

Marie contrived to escape from the drawing-room, and went into the library, where she could be alone. It happened to be next to the study, to which there were two doors, one opening into it, the other giving upon the passage. The sound of raised voices caught her ear and made her tremble as she hastily went to the other end of the room, so as not to overhear a conversation which was not meant for her ears; but the next moment she heard the far door of the study closed violently, and at the same time the one leading into the library flew open, and Colonel de St. Severan entered, his face all in a glow from anger and indignation. He started as he saw Marie, who ran to him, exclaiming—

"My father! What has happened?"

"Marie, my dear child, I did not expect to find you here," he said, putting his arms round her, and looking earnestly at her; "but perhaps it is better as it is. Henceforth you will teach your heart to forget *ce monsieur*. He is unworthy of you, and I have told him never to dare to address you again! My child, I know, will do her best to obey me when I tell her that she must think no more of him!"

Marie became pale as death. Her lips quivered as she tried to answer; but instead of words there burst from her a long, low sob, and she remained passive in his arms.

CHAPTER XI.

THE interview between Colonel de St. Severan and Mr. Barkley was short but stormy. That morning the former had called upon Lord Barkley to learn what were his true feelings with regard to his son's marriage.

Lord Barkley was a most plausible old gentleman, and liked to keep well with everybody; accordingly he bespattered Colonel de St. Severan with compliments, said that he himself found Mademoiselle Arbi charming, and that nothing grieved him more than being obliged to tell Edmund that if he married without getting a fortune of thirty or forty thousand pounds, he must leave the ancestral estate, in order to preserve it in the family, away from him; but were it not for their unfortunate embarrassments he would be only too delighted to receive Mademoiselle as his daughter-in-law.

Colonel de St. Severan thanked him and took his leave. Now that he had heard from Lord

Barkley's own lips how much he approved of
Marie personally, and that he left his son free to
marry her if he chose to brave the threat of the
family estate being left away from him, Colonel
de St. Severan felt himself authorised in making
the proposal to Mr. Barkley of which he had
spoken to Marie.

Unfortunately for Mr. Barkley he had been
out all the morning, and went to the de St.
Severans without having heard what had passed
between his father and Colonel de St. Severan, so
he was completely taken by surprise when the
latter called him into his study, and having
explained how it was that by chance he discovered
the attachment which existed between him and
Marie, he proceeded to relate all that Lord
Barkley had said to him; then in a concise but
cutting manner he blamed Mr. Barkley for his
conduct throughout the whole affair. He concluded by saying that it pained him deeply to
think that Marie should have bestowed her affec-
tions upon one who had acted towards her as Mr.
Barkley had done, but that she had wrung from
him a promise not to put any obstacle in the way of
her happiness, and in compliance with this promise
he named the fortune which he was ready to give
Marie, showing at the same time that he knew
such a portion would enable Mr. Barkley to marry

her—if he really loved her—independently of his father.

Mr. Barkley was not, as we said before, in a serene mood when he entered the study, and this speech of Colonel de St. Severan's worked him up almost into a passion. It was forcing him to do the very thing which he did not wish to do—to choose at once between love and mammon. To give up the latter and resolve to live on the thousand or so a year which his own and Marie's income would amount to, seemed to him too alarming a sacrifice. On the other hand he saw plainly that if he did not make it he must renounce Marie for ever, as he had no excuse to give for any further hesitation, save the true one of his unwillingness to run the risk of being a comparatively poor man all his life; after what his father had said he had not the courage to plead that fear of displeasing him was his motive.

He hated the colonel for placing him in such a position, and in vain he tried to think calmly how he could answer, until Colonel de St. Severan, tired of waiting for a reply, said—

"Your silence, I suppose, is a tacit acknowledgment that you have been merely trifling with Mademoiselle Arbi all this time ; but indeed it is only what one might have expected from the whole tenor of your past conduct."

This was like applying a lighted match to a train of gunpowder. Mr. Barkley lost all control of himself, accused Colonel de St. Severan of false dealing, in having gone secretly to speak about him to his father, and said many other things which, had he been master of himself, he would never have uttered. Colonel de St. Severan interrupted him in a voice of thunder, commanded him to leave his presence instantly, and never to dare to speak to him or Mademoiselle Arbi again. He pointed to the door, and Mr. Barkley—awed by the dignity of his manner—obeyed the gesture silently, quailing like a bold schoolboy before the great and just anger of his superior.

He rushed out of the house in a state of wild excitement, and, as the fates ordained, almost at the door he met some young Frenchmen of his acquaintance.

They said they were going to dine at the Trois Frères, and asked him to join them. Mr. Barkley, glad to have any company rather than that of his own thoughts, accepted the proposal, and away they went to the Palais Royal.

The repast was most *récherché*, and naturally the wines were in keeping with it. Mr. Barkley drank freely of them all, and especially of champagne, until his spirits became quite exuberant, and when *écarté* was suggested as a fitting wind-

up to the evening, he eagerly expressed his pleasure at the suggestion.   He played high and lost
considerable sums, but the more he lost the more
recklessly he played, and it was with difficulty that
his companions got him away from the card-table
in time to dress for the ambassador's ball, to which
they were all going.

It chanced that the Molyneuxes and Mr.
Barkley arrived about the same time, and he
secured Miss Molyneux for the next valse.   She
looked dazzlingly handsome in some sort of a
light-blue dress over white satin, and a necklace
of turquoise.   A buzz of admiration followed her
as she moved in her stately manner through the
crowd, leaning on her partner's arm, so that Mr.
Barkley began to feel that at least she would be a
wife that a man could be proud of; and the valse
finished the matter.   Excitement, champagne,
and that rapid dance all told upon him, and fired
his heart with a momentary fancy for Miss
Molyneux.   He made desperate love to her, proposed, and was sobered by her calm acceptation of
his offer.   Up to that moment he scarcely knew
what he was saying, but her cool answer and
suggestion that they should return to "papa"
made him fully sensible of what he had done.   It
was as if a pail of iced water had been thrown
over him, and he could scarcely help shivering as

he offered his arm to his affianced bride to lead her to her parents.

Mr. Barkley passed that night in all the torture of self-reproach. More than once, after he returned from the ambassador's, he attempted to write an apology to Colonel de St. Severan, but each time he tore up what he had written, feeling that it would look like a mockery to send an apology after that night's work, as he knew that of course the de St. Severans must hear of his engagement. When he did at last go to bed, he lay tossing on it with sleepless eyes and a racking headache as well as *heartache*.

The next morning he went into his father's room, about ten o'clock, looking so "*seedy*" and haggard that the latter exclaimed—

"Why, Edmund, you must have supped after the ball last night. You certainly look as if you had a good bout of it."

"Such an one, sir, as I shall never forget, only it was *at* the ball and not after it," answered his son; "and I have come to tell you that my happiness is destroyed for life, but your wishes are gratified. Miss Molyneux is my affianced wife. I hope *she* has money enough for you!"

"My dear Edmund, you amaze me! I should indeed have been delighted to hear of your engagement if you did not speak of it in this extraordinary manner. Surely I did not insist upon your proposing to Miss Molyneux."

" No, but you drove me to desperation by opposing my marriage with the woman I love. I behaved like a scoundrel to her and to Colonel de St. Severan ; then to escape from my own thoughts I drank and gambled until I was half mad with excitement, and in that state I proposed to Miss Molyneux."

" Don't flurry yourself about it, my dear boy ; under the circumstances, we can explain away anything a little too tender which you may have said to Miss Molyneux. I should be very sorry if you were to marry a girl whom you don't like ; and as for the de St. Severan affair, I don't understand what you mean. I saw the colonel yesterday morning and explained everything to him. Why, we parted like the dearest friends in the world ! "

" I know it, sir, but I have seen Colonel de St. Severan since, and——, but, no, I cannot speak of it. Now, with regard to Miss Molyneux," he continued, hurriedly ; " you are mistaken in supposing that I merely said something too tender to her which could be explained away. I told you expressly that she was my affianced wife. I was not drunk enough—would that I had been—to talk nonsense ; only enough to act like a madman.

I proposed formally to Miss Molyneux, and she
as—no far more—formally accepted me, and
marched me up to 'papa.' As to not liking her,
why I could no more like or dislike her than I
could a beautiful piece of marble, so I may as well
marry her as anybody else, since I am not to have
the only one whom I love."

"Still, Edmund, it appears to me that you
would do well to think a little more about this
before you go any further."

"It's all very well for you, sir, to talk in this
way now after you have driven me into it. I
have twice said that I can't draw back unless I
behave in the same manner to Miss Molyneux as
I have done to that little angel, Marie Arbi. But
let there be an end to all discussion. The die is
cast. We must go to old Molyneux this morning,
and you may make any arrangements you like
with him, but I leave Paris to-morrow. I am not
going to stay here to be a lasting insult to my
poor lost darling. At what hour will you come
with me to my future father-in-law?"

"At twelve, if you like, my dear fellow; but I
am really unhappy about the manner in which
you take this up. I wish something could be
done to get you out of it."

"But nothing can be done, sir, and the
greatest kindness you can show me is to say no

more about it.   We must only make the best of a
bad case.   At twelve I will meet you in the
coffee-room."

So saying Mr. Barkley returned to his own
room and began to dress.   .

The Molyneuxes left Paris a few days after this
and went to London, whither Lord Barkley and
his son had preceded them.   The latter urged his
father to get the settlements drawn up as quickly
as possible, as he declared that the shorter time he
had to sustain the lover's part towards his " marble bride" elect, the better it would be for them
both, and he undertook to get Miss Molyneux to
name an early day for the wedding.   Accordingly
it was fixed for the second week in April.

Towards the end of the month—February—the
Barkleys left London for Ireland, on the plea of
seeing that all the preparations for receiving the
bride were being properly executed.   Mr. Barkley
however was to return to London in a fortnight or
three weeks.   In the meantime he, as well as his
father, was delighted to get home to their beautiful place, and the attractions of a country life;
even the old lord was still a keen sportsman.

A short time after their return there was to be
a meet in the neighbourhood, and some eight or
ten gentlemen were invited to dine and sleep at
Barkley Castle the night before.   It was a sort of

farewell bachelor party, which Mr. Barkley induced his father to give. There was a good deal of joking about the approaching marriage, but the only answer which Mr. Barkley deigned to give to all the questions which were asked about his "ladye love" was—"When you see her you'll all acknowledge that I have imported something worth *looking* at."

Lord Barkley, however, saw by the impatient twitching of his lip how disagreeable the subject was to him, and although later in the evening he became boisterously gay, sang comic songs, and related many a good story, his father felt that his gaiety was forced, and more than ever did he regret the hastiness with which he had entered into the engagement with Miss Molyneux; yet he said to himself, "Perhaps it is better so. Once married he'll be proud of having such a magnificent looking wife, and they'll get on right well, I daresay. If he does not marry he would always have a hankering after that little Marie; not that I am a bit astonished at it, for she is a sweet little creature, and the other is so stiff and cold; but it would be ruin for him not to get a large fortune, so it's all as well that he is going to be settled, —only I wish with all my heart that the poor fellow seemed to like the idea of it a little better."

After this soliloquy his lordship sought his

couch ; nevertheless, as he rose next morning and donned his hunting suit, he could not shake off an unaccountable feeling of sadness and remorse about " Edmund's " coming marriage, and the latter happening to go in to him to ask some question relative to the starting, he said, laying his hand upon his shoulder—

" Come, boy, you and I must not go out to-day with any ill-will between us."

" How now, father ; surely you are not growing nervous ?"

" No, Edmund, that's quite out of my line ; but before we go I want to hear you say that you bear me no grudge for opposing you about Miss Arbi. You must feel that it was only your own interest that I had at heart in so doing. I shall be dead and gone in a few years at farthest, but you would have been a ruined man all your life if I had forwarded a marriage between her and you."

Mr. Barkley winced at Marie's name and turned away his head, but when his father ceased speaking he answered gently, although sorrowfully—

" I do not doubt that you acted for the best, father ; but was wealth worth the sacrifice of happiness ? I, however, as well as you, helped to make the sacrifice, therefore I cannot blame you more than I do myself, or, God knows ! half as much ; so if it's any satisfaction to you to hear me say so, I

bear you no grudge about it, father. My marriage
with Miss Molyneux is my own work, and I must
make the best of it."

" If the thought of it really makes you unhappy,
Edmund," exclaimed Lord Barkley, struck by the
despondency of his son's tone, "let us try to
break it off even now."

" Why break it off, father, and at the expense
of my honour too, unless you are willing to try
and win back for me the girl whom I love?"

Mr. Barkley's eyes kindled for a moment as he
looked half-questioningly at Lord Barkley, who
felt almost tempted to answer, "Yes, I *will* get
her back for you, and make you happy, my boy,
if I can." But Mammon whispered, "What!
for a young man's foolish dream of love will you
let your broad acres pass away from the family?"
and he replied, looking out of the window to avoid
meeting his son's earnest gaze—" True, Edmund,
your marriage could not be broken off now, as you
say, except at the expense of your honour ; and,
after all, Miss Molyneux *is* gloriously handsome."

It was with difficulty that his son refrained from
making an exclamation of impatience, but he did
refrain, and left the room, merely saying, " I
suppose it is nearly time for breakfast?"

Some hours afterwards how glad Mr. Barkley
was that he had so restrained his impatience.

CHAPTER XII

IT was such a morning as the old song describes:

"A southerly wind and a cloudy sky
Proclaim a hunting morning;"

and a troop of about a dozen gentlemen rode gaily
out of the courtyard, revelling in the enjoyment
of expected pleasure. They were not disappointed
in regard to the hunt itself; but a fatal accident,
which occurred just at its close, threw a gloom
over the day.

Reynard was making a last struggle for his life
as the hunt galloped up to the yawning fence
over which they had to pass in order to be in at
the "death." There was an up-bank on the side
next to the riders, and on the other a gaping
dyke, brimfull of water. The two foremost
horses took it gallantly, but the third jumped
short, lost his footing, and slipped back into the
water. His rider, however, succeeded in throw-
ing himself off, and he clung to the side of the

ditch, shouting at the same time to those behind
to give him room. Unfortunately, at that very
moment a horse appeared at the top of the bank,
and, startled by the shout just as he was rising
for the spring, he swerved, reared, and fell back-
wards from the bank, crushing his hapless rider
under him.

The rider was Lord Barkley; and the gentlemen who immediately followed him reined in
their horses and sprang to the ground to assist
him. They had succeeded in getting the horse
from over him, when they beheld his son standing
on the top of the bank with a horror-stricken
expression of countenance, and his clothes all
saturated with water. Mr. Barkley was one of
the two first horsemen who had so gallantly taken
the leap ; but the shout of the man who fell made
him turn round in his saddle, and he saw his
father's horse swerve and fall!

A low cry escaped his lips as he glanced at the
ditch to see if it were possible to take it from the
side upon which he found himself; but even at
such a moment he saw that it was almost impossible that any horse could do it, and dismounting
hurriedly, he threw himself into the water, crossed,
and scrambled up the bank, where, as we have
seen, he stood looking with horror on the scene
before him. But it was only for a moment that

he stood there; the next, he was kneeling beside his father, and supporting his head on his knee.

The only sign of life which Lord Barkley gave was to moan whenever they attempted to move him, until one of the gentlemen brought some water in his hat, and sprinkled it over him. He then opened his eyes, and recognising his son, he pressed his hand, and murmured, " Good-bye, my boy; it's all over with me, but be happy in your own way." The rest was lost in indistinct sounds.

Mr. Barkley bent his head lower and lower, until his dark locks mingled with his father's grey hair; and the gentlemen stood by silently, not venturing to disturb the mourner even to ask what could be done.

A poor tenant, however, went up to him, and, touching him on the shoulder, said with rough good nature, " Come now, Misther Barkley, be a man, and don't take on so. Shure, maybe the good auld lord will come too, afther all; and isn't it a quare thing for yer honours to be all standing there and niver thinking what could be done to rekiver him. Faix, and its close to B——town that we are, and what w'd ail a few boys like me-self to take a twist over to it and bring back a stretcher or something of that soort for to carry his lordship? Shure, and your honour's own

docther lives there too; and couldn't we bring
him along wid us?"

"You are right, my good friend," answered
Mr. Barkley, raising his head; "I ought to have
thought of that. Please, then, to go; but on
horseback; and ride at full speed."

When the doctor arrived, he tried to examine his poor old friend, in order to see what
injuries he had received; but every touch seemed
to give him such pain that the doctor desisted,
and said, "We had better get him placed on the
stretcher and carried as gently as possible to my
house; then we can see better what is to be
done."

When the poor sufferer had been carefully
raised and laid on the stretcher, the sad proces-
sion moved slowly on, Mr. Barkley and the doctor
walking by the side of the bier, which four stal-
wart countrymen carried.

Before setting out, however, the former said in
a broken voice to those about him, "Gentlemen,
I am most grateful to you for your kindness. I
cannot speak about it now, but I shall never forget it."

The same night—and little more than twelve
hours after they all started in "gallant array"
from Barkley Castle—Lord Barkley's spirit was
at rest. From the first the doctor had seen that

there was no hope of recovery, but he was able to do much towards alleviating the dying man's sufferings, who, although unable to speak, was evidently sensible to the last, and he received the Church's sacraments with deep emotion.

Mr. Barkley—or rather now Lord Barkley—was so stunned by the manner and suddenness of his father's death, that he could scarcely realise the fact that he who, a few hours ago, rode by his side in the full enjoyment of health and spirits, was now a corpse; and the only words which he spoke for long after death had taken place were, "Thank God, 'twas not in anger that I spoke to him last!"

Next day the body was removed to Barkley Castle, and there laid out in state until the funeral, which was fixed for the fourth day after death.

Lord Barkley begged his brother-in-law, Mr. Penton, to arrange everything without appealing to him, as he felt too confused to be able to think.

Mr. Penton consequently acted on his own judgment as to whom he ought to invite for the funeral, and above all others he thought it right to ask Mr. Molyneux (the present lord's future father-in-law), although he thought it most unlikely that he would come. But on the contrary, he received a telegram to say that Mr. Molyneux would arrive at Barkley Castle the evening before the funeral.

When this was told to Lord Barkley he appeared to be much agitated ; and in answer to his sister's eager question as to whether her husband had done wrong in inviting Mr. Molyneux, he said, "No, Maria ; I am sure that George only did what ought to have been done, although I would rather not see Mr. Molyneux just yet."

The late lord's dying words to his son, " be happy in your own way," made a deep impression upon him, for it was an acknowledgment at the last moment that his father regretted having urged him to sacrifice happiness for wealth, and that he did not wish the sacrifice to be completed. Thus during the solemn hours that he watched beside the dead he could not help being struck by the greatness of the revelations which approaching death makes, even to a man who has toiled all his life for wealth, and was ready to give up everything in order to obtain it. And now, too, as he viewed his own conduct with the strong light of eternity shining upon it, he saw all its weakness and want of truth. He had acted treacherously both to the girl whom he loved and to the one to whom he was affianced, and with shame and sorrow he felt that however unhappy his life might be henceforth he must blame himself as the *chief* cause of it.

Remorse and unhappiness, thus added to the natural grief which he felt for a parent who had loved him well though not wisely, made him look so haggard and worn as he stood with blanched cheeks and trembling lips, looking upon the closing of the vault over his father, that Mr. Molyneux went up to him and tried to lead him away. "Come, Edmund," said he, "let your second father help to console you for the loss which you have just sustained. My daughter's husband will be nearly as dear to me as a child of my own. Only treat me as a father, and you will find that I am such to you by affection though not by nature."

For the sake of his manhood Lord Barkley struggled hard to repress the tears which rose to his eyes as Mr. Molyneux spoke, and brushing them hastily away, he said sadly and humbly, "Mr. Molyneux, I am unworthy of your goodness,—I have deceived you all. You must let me make a full confession to you to-morrow morning, when I shall be more composed than I am now. You can never again think well of me after you have heard it, but it is the only reparation in my power to make, and you shall at least know me for what I am, before anything irrevocable has been done."

Mr. Molyneux started, and was on the point of demanding an explanation at once, but as he looked at Lord Barkley walking beside him with drooping head, and wrapped in the mourner's garb of deep woe, he refrained through respect for unaffected grief, and determined to wait as patiently as he could until the time named.

Mr. Penton acted as his brother-in-law's deputy in doing the honours of the house, as Lord Barkley retired to his own room immediately after the funeral and remained there all day. The next morning, however, about eleven, he sent to Mr. Molyneux to say that if it suited his convenience he would be glad to see him in the library.

He repaired thither at once, and as he entered Lord Barkley said, "Mr. Molyneux, I do not offer you my hand until you have heard all that I am going to tell you, as perhaps you would not wish to shake hands with me, were you aware of what my conduct has been. You shall hear in as few words as possible how miserable and dishonourable a part weakness and habitual self-indulgence may lead a naturally honourable man to act. The shock of my poor father's sudden death, and the sad time for reflection which has followed it, have made me feel how shamefully I have behaved towards you and your daughter, and that at least I ought to tell you what have been and are my feelings towards her. May I count upon your forbearance to listen to me without interruption ? "

Mr. Molyneux assented, and Lord Barkley then shortly but fully detailed to him all that had passed from the time he had seen Marie— without naming her of course—up to the night when he proposed to Miss Molyneux, adding, "Now, Mr. Molyneux, that you have heard all, I have only to say I am quite ready to fulfil my engagement. I think I could promise to be a good and kind though not a loving husband to your daughter. I would take care never to look again upon the face of her whom I love, and endeavour to efface her image from my heart. What more can I do under the circumstances? And I think that at least it was truer to tell you all this than to continue to deceive you. I believe, too, from what I know of Miss Molyneux's character, that she would be quite satisfied with the sincere respect and affection which I feel for her. I should be the only sufferer, and fully do I acknowledge that I deserve any punishment which may be inflicted upon me. Even you cannot blame me more bitterly than I have blamed myself, and there is no humiliation or expiation that you could

impose upon me which I would not willingly
accept. In the name, then, of your old friend
—my poor father—who through too indulgent
affection helped to make me what I am, I
ask you to try not to think too harshly of me.
Do not even in your own mind brand me as one
utterly devoid of honour and principle, but say
what you wish me to do."

Mr. Molyneux was one of the kindest, not to say
most soft-hearted men that ever lived, and Lord
Barkley's air of deep suffering and self-abasement
touched him even in the midst of his anger and
indignation. He thought of his own dead son,
who would now be just about the same age as the
poor culprit before him, and pushing away his
chair he walked up and down the room muttering
to himself.

No one knew more thoroughly his daughter's
cold, proud character than he did, or so mourned
over it; and his grief for his passionate, affectionate boy had been redoubled and perpetuated
by the feeling that he could find no real comfort
in his remaining child.

The more he looked at Lord Barkley, the more
did the memory of his own Edmund knock at his
heart and intercede for indulgence towards the
errors of a loving nature, which weakness and
over indulgence had led astray; and knowing his

daughter's character as he did, he felt that it would be punishing him too severely to ask him to fulfil his engagement with her whilst his young heart yearned for one who was evidently *not* a statue. Nevertheless he could not but feel indignant at the manner in which his daughter had been treated, and at last he said, sternly—

" Lord Barkley, you were right when you said that your conduct had merited for you the misery of being married to one woman whilst you loved another, and if I believed that the breaking off of this marriage would cause my daughter a moment's deep pain, I should not hesitate to require you to fulfil your engagement ; but she is not one who would allow herself to *love* any man until after he was her husband, and I know that I have only to tell her that from your own showing you were unworthy of her, and her self-respect will enable her to bear the separation without much regret. I will not, therefore, take upon myself to inflict upon you the fate which you deserve. You may, then, consider yourself released from the engagement, and I shall never say more than is necessary as to why this marriage was broken off ; but you cannot object to my letting it be understood that it was your own conduct which caused it, and henceforth let us be as strangers to each other. For

the sake of my dear lost boy, whose schoolfellow
you were, rather than for that of the hardly true
friend who urged you to treat us as you have
done, have I been thus lenient to you, and I do
not think that you could have asked more."

"*I* have asked more! God knows I had no
right to expect such indulgence as you have
shown me," answered Lord Barkley, raising his
head, and Mr. Molyneux saw that his face was
marked by traces of tears such as a man rarely
sheds. After a moment's pause Lord Barkley
resumed—

"Your reproaches I could have borne better
than such forbearance,—it is indeed heaping coals
of fire upon my head. I dare not hope that you
will ever take my hand in friendship again, but
whilst I live no son of your own could look upon
you with deeper feelings of gratitude and respect
than I do. Good-bye, and perhaps the spirit of
your own lost son will plead for his weak, erring
companion as it did to-day, and at last win back
for him one ray of the old kindly feeling of
former days."

Lord Barkley looked so dejected and humbled
that Mr. Molyneux had not the heart to leave
him thus coldly, and turning hastily round from
the door, which he had almost reached, he
grasped his hand, saying, "Good-bye, boy; I

dare say you'll make as good a man as any of us after all."

He gave the hand which he held a cordial shake and then hastened out of the room.

•

CHAPTER XIII.

Lord Barkley being thus relieved from his engagement to Miss Molyneux, felt like a prisoner just set free, who rejoices in his newly-recovered freedom, although the remembrance of the acts which riveted the chains of bondage round his neck still fills his heart with shame and sorrow; and he set to work in earnest to try and make amends for all past self-indulgence and extravagance.

For the three first months which followed his father's death, he applied himself with energy to the examination of his affairs. He found them in a dreadful state of confusion, and, totally unaccustomed as he was to business, it seemed to him almost impossible that he could ever get through the masses of ill-kept accounts which lay before him, and his evil genius—indolence—more than once suggested to him that it would have been unnecessary to do so had he married Miss Molyneux; but at such moments he had only to look back and recall his misery during the time of his engagement to her, in order to feel that any-thing—even breaking his head over accounts—was better than that; and then with renewed vigour he would pore over the long lines of figures, think-ing to himself, "I would willingly go through all this if I could only hope that Marie was not lost to me for ever; yet even on chance I will labour on, and endeavour to show that I am some-what less unworthy of her than I was."

Lord Barkley was naturally clever; all he had ever wanted was application and energy, and these were now lent to him by sorrow for the past, and hope, however faint it might be, for the future. Notwithstanding many a weary hour, when his courage wavered, and he felt half inclined to abandon the task which he had set himself to do, he did at last succeed in making himself com-pletely master of his position. He then saw that it was possible to retrieve the property without selling himself for a large fortune in marriage, but it could only be done by—what appeared to him—strict economy and attention to business.

"I *will* do it," he exclaimed one evening, as he locked up the papers which he had been studying. "If Colonel de St. Severan can be induced to give me Marie, we could live abroad for some years, and everything would go swimmingly. But how

can I dare to address him? I suppose he would
neither see me nor receive a letter from me. And
Marie—ah! *she* would not be too hard on me if I
could only plead my own cause to her. But again,
how am I to see her? I have it! Flora Adair
can help me if she will; she can intercede for me
with the de St. Severans; and the old colonel likes
her particularly, Marie has often told me so. But
will she help me? God knows! However, *she*
will not refuse to see me, and perhaps when she
hears all she may be persuaded to aid me when I
am doing my utmost to repair the past. Without Marie I have no motive for exertion, and if
she is really lost to me, then I am indeed lost. But
I will try whether Flora Adair cannot be moved
to help and save me. I will go to Dublin to-
morrow, and see if she is like so many others, who
sternly refuse to assist the fallen when they try to
rise to better things."

The next day, before the usual visiting hour,
Flora Adair was much surprised when Lord
Barkley's card was handed to her, and the servant
said that the gentleman earnestly begged Miss
Adair would see him, even though she did not
generally receive visitors when Mrs. Adair was out.
Flora hesitated a little, but finally said, "Well
then, show him up."

When Lord Barkley entered the room, he was

startled by the brilliant delicacy of her complexion, and exclaimed, " Miss Adair, have you been ill?"

" I am not very well, Lord Barkley, and am scarcely able to receive any but my most intimate friends; however, I did not like to refuse you, as you asked so particularly to see me," she answered coldly, for she had never forgiven his lordship for his conduct to Marie.

" I am truly sorry to hear that you are not well, Miss Adair, and I am most grateful to you for not refusing to see me, for you, if any one, can help to restore me to happiness and peace of mind. Will you listen to the confession of my sins against one who is dear to you, but dearer far to me; and then, if you deem me worthy of forgiveness, will you try to obtain it for me?"

" I will hear whatever your lordship wishes to tell me, but I can make no promise for my after conduct."

Lord Barkley then gave her a clear and full account of all that he had done from the time he went to Paris until the present; in no way did he extenuate or gloss over any of his faults, or dwell upon his courageous determination during the last three months to battle with the difficulties of his position and conquer them. Never had he appeared to Flora in so favourable a light as now, when he humbly exposed all his past weakness, but showed by his conduct since his father's death that he did possess energy and strength of mind sufficient to repent and begin quite a new life; and he had gained her as an intercessor even before he concluded by saying, "If Marie would trust me again with the blessing of her love, the work of amendment which has been begun in me would be perfected: for then I should have the strongest of motives to repair the past, and she, I do believe, would be angelic enough to forgive me all my weakness and infidelity to her. But I dare not venture to address Colonel de St. Severan, —I could not expect from him any of that indulgence which she, in the plenitude of her goodness, might grant me. If I wrote to him I suppose he would send me back my letter unread, but if you, Miss Adair, would deign to help me —if you would write to Colonel de St. Severan and Marie in my favour, and enclose to each of them a letter from me, it would at least enable me to plead my own cause. I know how great was your contempt for my weakness even in Florence, and then I had not behaved half so badly as I did afterwards; but what more can I do than mourn over my great faults, and try to rise to better things? Will you, then, aid me in that attempt to rise, for without Marie I have no hope?"

"I will help you as far as I can, Lord Barkley, answered Flora cordially, as she looked fixedly at him, and marked the worn, anxious expression of his countenance; "and now for the first time do I think you worthy of Marie. There is no fault so great that true repentance cannot efface it, and I know that dear, gentle Marie will not be too hard upon you, although you well-nigh broke her heart. Your engagement to Miss Molyneux was a cruel wound to her confiding nature; but 'let the dead past bury its dead.' 1 will spare no exertion to induce Colonel de St. Severan to relent towards you; and Marie, I dare say, will be a still warmer and a more powerful advocate for you than any one else. So send me the letters, and I will write at once; and now I must ask you to leave me, for I am very tired; yet you have done me good. To try to make Marie happy is something pleasant to do and to think about."

"I know no words strong enough to express my gratitude to you, Miss Adair. You have been to me like a good angel, bidding me hope that my repentance may win my pardon, even while suffering yourself, for your voice, everything, tells me that you, too, are suffering. May Heaven reward you for your goodness to me!" He took her hand, raised it to his lips, and left her, promising to send her the letters that evening.

As soon as Flora received them she lost no time in forwarding them to the de St. Severans, accompanied by a few lines from herself, both to Marie and Colonel de St. Severan. And while these important letters are passing through the post, we shall precede them to the chateau, and learn how their contents are likely to be received by its occupants. . . .

Colonel de St. Severan's mother was English, and from her he had learned a somewhat less matter-of-fact idea of marriage than the generality of French people entertain, and therefore he was wonderfully indulgent towards Marie's grief when her *love* match was broken off; nevertheless he *was* a Frenchman by birth and education, and he considered that the best cure for that grief would be to find her a handsome young husband, endowed with all the desirable advantages of position and fortune—"*enfin un établissement convenable sous tous les rapports.*"

Shortly after their return to the country, which took place in Easter week, Colonel de St. Severan was overjoyed at receiving a visit from an old friend and neighbour, the Comte de Morlaix, who came to propose an alliance between his eldest son, le Comte Charles de Morlaix, and Marie.

He cordially assured his friend that nothing would make him happier than to see his dear

Marie united to so excellent and charming a young man as le Comte Charles, adding that he would let him know his adopted daughter's sentiments on the subject in a day or two, but that doubtless she would feel only too deeply gratified by the honour which the Comte and Comtesse de Morlaix conferred upon her by thus desiring to welcome her into the family as their daughter-in-law.

The Comte de Morlaix then took his leave, after having made a profusion of complimentary speeches, well satisfied in thinking that he had obtained for his son a pretty, an amiable, and a wealthy bride.

Colonel de St. Severan was equally pleased with the prospect of presenting the handsome, gay young Comte to Marie as her future husband, and felt quite convinced that it would effectually banish any regret which she might *still* feel for Lord Barkley.

Accordingly he hastened to find Marie, in order to communicate this flattering proposal to her; but to his great disappointment she had no sooner heard it than she began to cry, and sobbingly declared that she would never marry, and only wanted to be allowed to live always with her " *cher père.*"

Colonel de St. Severan treated all this as girlish

sentimentality, and told her to talk it all over with her good old friend, Monsieur le Curé, who would advise her as to what she ought to do.

Poor, gentle, yielding little Marie! how could she resist the persuasion and the reasoning of her beloved adopted father and the good Curé? She knew not how to answer when in measured accents they spoke of the dreadful consequences which any indulgence in romantic feelings might lead to, and counselled her to accept—as a safe-guard against the dangerous inclination of her own heart for one who was about to become the husband of another—the pleasing and pious young Comte who now sought her in marriage. She could not, as we have said, reason with them about it; but from her heart burst forth the cry, " Oh, no ! It cannot be right to marry the Comte Charles when I love another better than I can love him."

" Poor child ! " replied the Curé compassion-ately; " we only want to make you happy, and your loving father by adoption will not press you for an answer. In the meantime you can see Monsieur le Comte Charles now and then, and think over all that we have said to you."

Marie at length consented to see her proposed suitor occasionally, but only on this condition, that he, or at least his father, should be told the whole truth. That is to say, that she was still smarting under the pain which a final separation from one whom she had loved caused her, and that consequently she did not feel inclined to entertain the thought of marrying at all. Nevertheless, in compliance with the wishes of her *cher père*, she would, if *Monsieur le Comte de Morlaix* still wished it, receive the visits of his son in order that she might become better acquainted with him. But these visits were to be considered strictly as visits of friendship until after the expiration of two months, when she should have completed her twenty-first year, and then she would say if they were to assume another character, or cease altogether.

These conditions were accepted, for the de Morlaix were really most anxious to win Marie for their son, and they had little doubt of his making a favourable impression upon the refractory young lady.

Marie was far too timid to assert her own sense of right by saying definitely, "I will not give my hand without my heart; for surely God cannot call upon me to swear falsely—to swear an allegiance to one for whom I have not even a very strong feeling of preference."

She longed to escape from this proposed marriage; but when she saw that every one around

her looked upon her disinclination to it as a wicked
indulgence in forbidden memories, she began to
doubt herself, and to suppose that although she
could not understand it, it must be wrong of her
to refuse the Comte Charles. Her only hope of
support was from Flora Adair; and she wrote
her a long history of it all, begging her to say
if *she* too thought it right for her to marry the
Comte Charles; "for," she added, candidly, "I
believe it is true to say that it is the memory of
what I once felt for another which makes me
wish to refuse him. He is very good and kind,
and had I never known Edmund, I dare say I
should have married him just because he is so
good and kind, and because *mon cher père* wishes
it. But as it is—— Flora, what shall I do?
The thought of this marriage is hateful to me
now."

Flora's answer, however, destroyed her last
hope of support. It ran thus:—

"MY POOR DARLING MIGNONNE,

"I must not dare to advise you at such
a time as the present, when peace, happiness,
everything, depends upon your decision. I have
no right to come between you and your
adopted father, Colonel de St. Severan, and his
friends. They have advised you, and now your

own heart and conscience can alone decide the question. One word only will I say,—no *man's* counsel is infallible ; and outside the Church's definitions of right and wrong, our conscience is the only code by which God will judge us. Trust to Him alone, and, under Him, to your own sense of right, and you cannot go wrong.

" Write to me often, and tell me how you feel as the time for your decision approaches. But you must never ask me to give any opinion about it. Do not think it cold and unkind of me, dearest, thus to throw you back upon yourself, and leave you to stand alone in this crisis of your life. Heaven knows how much it costs me to act so ; but I cannot do otherwise. Colonel de St. Severan would naturally resent any interference on my part; so in honour I am bound to be silent.

" Good-bye, then, dearest ; and may God direct you.

" Ever your affectionate

" FLORA ADAIR."

After the receipt of this letter Marie felt more unhappy than ever. Flora's words, " Trust to God alone, and, under Him, to your own sense of right," simply told her that she must act on her own responsibility ; for she could not suppose that

God would send down an angel to tell her what she ought to do.

In vain she tried to conquer her repugnance to the idea of marrying. But when they said to her that this was a temptation and a clinging to the memory of one whom she had no longer any right to love, she felt that she had not the courage to say, "I will not marry."

At length she began to look upon her union with the Comte Charles as a sort of fate, from which she could not escape by any act of her own. Yet she prayed day after day that, if it were God's holy will, the marriage might never take place.

Thus time glided on, slowly and sadly for Marie, and yet too quickly also; for it brought nearer and nearer the dreaded day when she was to give her final answer.

One soft, hazy June morning, as she sat in an arbour with Colonel de St. Severan, he said, " *Eh bien! mon enfant*, we are not far from your birthday, and then I hope you will make us all happy by allowing your *fiançailles* to be celebrated."

" But I need not give my answer until the very day, *mon père*," murmured Marie, bending low over the work in her hand.

"Certainly not, my child," answered Colonel de St. Severan. " I promised not to ask for one until then. I cannot help hoping, however, that so charming and virtuous a young man as Comte Charles has succeeded in making you feel how much happier you will be as his honoured wife than in rejecting him and yielding to unauthorised recollections of a married man, as no doubt Lord Barkley is by this time. Nevertheless, Marie, you know that you are free to act as you will. I do not desire you under pain of my displeasure to accept him; but I shall be sorry if it be otherwise, and a little disappointed in my dear child." He laid his hand fondly on her head, whilst she struggled to keep down the sobs which were rising in her throat.

Just then a servant entered with some letters on a salver. Colonel de St. Severan took them up, read the addresses, and placing before Marie an unusually large envelope, he said gaily, "There, little one, is a volume from your nice Irish friend. Just look how thick it is, too! Why, it will give you something to do to read all that. And I, too, must see what my correspondents have to say to me."

Not many minutes had passed when Colonel de St. Severan was startled by a joyful cry from Marie. "I am saved—saved—what joy!—what happiness! Read, *mon père.*" In her right hand she held up before him Flora's open letter,

and in her left another, upon which she gazed
with rapture. But the reaction was too great for
Marie's strength, and she burst into so violent a
fit of crying that Colonel de St. Severan was
obliged to take her into the house before even he
had time to read a line of the letter which had
caused all this extraordinary agitation; but he
guessed that in some way or other it must be
connected with Lord Barkley, and the very
thought of it enraged him.

Madame de St. Severan happened to be passing
through the hall as they entered, and Colonel de
St. Severan hastily consigned Marie to her care,
and shut himself up in his study. By the same
post Flora wrote to Marie and Colonel de St.
Severan, enclosing Lord Barkley's respective
letters to each of them; but the one addressed to
Colonel de St. Severan, being mixed up among
several other letters, had escaped his notice until
he read her note to Marie, in which she spoke of
having also written to him. He then eagerly
looked for it, and, having found it, tore open the
envelope and read her letter and Lord Barkley's
as attentively as his increasing indignation would
allow him.

Lord Barkley's letter was so frank and open in
its acknowledgment of past unworthiness, and so
humble in its appeal for forgiveness, that Flora

hoped it might soften Colonel de St. Severan's
anger towards him; and her own letter closed
with these words—"You cannot any longer
doubt Lord Barkley's love for Marie. Think
what it must have cost a man like him, and in
his position, to humble himself as he has done
both to you and Mr. Mólyneux; yet he did it for
her sake. And I need not say that she loves
him. You know it well, since you thought, when
he was engaged to another, that she was bound to
guard even against the memory of that love by
making a marriage of duty, to say the least of it.
Dreadful as it appeared to me that she should be
induced to marry in this way, I forced myself to
be silent until I learned that he whom she loved
was free, and ready to make any atonement in
order to obtain her hand. So now, dear Colonel
de St. Severan, I hope you will pardon me for
becoming Lord Barkley's mediatrix. Marie needs
no intercessor with you; your own deep affection
for her will be a far more powerful advocate in
favour of her happiness than anything which I
could say. It will not let you see her suffer
very long when you know that it is in your
power to make her happy by forgiving her lover
and receiving him as your adopted son-in-law."

Colonel de St. Severan, however, passionately
declared in his own mind, when he finished reading

these letters, that he would never consent to give
Marie to a man who had treated her as Lord
Barkley had done. Repentance came too late; and,
so far as he was concerned, he would sternly reject
him. He was just about to write a few chilling
lines to Flora, re-enclosing Lord Barkley's letter,
and expressing his astonishment that he should
have had the presumption to address him, when
he was called away on business which obliged
him to absent himself from home for a few hours.

When he returned he was met at the door by
Marie, who, all radiant with joy, threw herself into
his arms, and gaily whispered, mimicking his words
in the morning, "Now, *mon père*, I am quite ready
to make you all happy by allowing my *fiançailles* to
be celebrated as soon as you will. I will not even
claim the fulfilment of your promise to wait for
my answer until my birthday. See what a difference a name makes; now that I may be affianced
to Edmund instead of to Charles, I ask for no
delay. Ah! how happy I am!"

"Marie! I am ashamed of you!" exclaimed
Colonel de St. Severan, pushing her from him.
"If you had the slightest sense of maidenly
dignity you would consider it an insult that Lord
Barkley should dare to address you again, instead
of showing this unseemly joy and of heedlessly
rejecting the honour of becoming the Comte Charles

de Morlaix's wife in order to give yourself to one
who cast you off! But I will save you if I can.
By this post I shall send back Lord Barkley's
letter to Miss Adair, requesting that the subject
may never be named to me again."

This was a sad check to Marie, to whom the
possibility of his not forgiving her lover had never
occurred. She only thought of all he had suffered,
and longed to be able to console him and make
him forget the unhappy past. But Colonel de St.
Severan's words rudely dispelled this delicious
dream, and the only concession which her prayers
and tears could win from him was a promise that
he would not send Lord Barkley's letter back to
him; but he persisted in writing to Flora, and
begged of her to convey to her friend, Lord
Barkley, his decided refusal even to tolerate the
idea of his becoming Marie's husband, and, as a
favour, he asked Flora not in any way to
encourage Marie in this misplaced affection.

Colonel de St. Severan allowed Marie to see the
letter, and even consented that she should add a
few lines. She accordingly wrote, with trembling
fingers—" Tell Edmund, dearest Flora, that I
have forgiven and forgotten everything but his
love for me; and would—so gladly!—prove to
him how fully it is returned by giving myself to
him at once. But, as you see from the above, my

dear father refuses his consent to our marriage;
and I could not be so ungrateful as to marry in
the face of his prohibition. I will never, however, marry any one else. Thank God! they
cannot persuade me now that it is wrong to love
him; and if he thinks me worth waiting for, we
may yet be happy. My dear father, I feel sure,
is too fond of me not to relent at last. Pray,
then, *ma Flore*, for thy Mignonne!"

Colonel de St. Severan frowned as he read these˙
lines, and folding up the letter, he said, "Delude
not yourself with false hopes, Marie. You can
of course marry Lord Barkley if you choose, but
it must ever be against my consent."

In spite of this, three months had not passed
when Flora Adair received a letter from Marie,
saying that she thought Colonel de St. Severan
was half inclined to yield; and if Lord Barkley
were to try the bold stroke of coming over and
seeking a personal interview with him, she hoped
all would terminate happily.

Her hope was realised. Colonel de St. Severan
had seen during these last few weeks that there
was no chance of inducing Marie to marry
according to his wishes now that Lord Barkley
was free,—now that they could no longer urge
that she was bound to forget *him* and become the
wife of the Comte Charles; and that consequently

he was only making her suffer to no purpose by continuing to refuse his consent to her wishes. So, when Lord Barkley unexpectedly presented himself before him, and pleaded his cause humbly and earnestly, as he had already done in writing, Colonel de St. Severan yielded, after a fair show of resistance, and led the grateful and happy Lord Barkley to Marie, to receive from her lips the ratification of his pardon. And to her tender mercies we may surely leave him without fearing that she will inflict any severe penance on him for his past wanderings.

CHAPTER XIV.

WE said in our last chapter that when Lord Barkley saw Flora Adair he was startled by her delicate appearance, therefore we may infer that time, which a poet has called " the only comforter when the heart hath bled," had not been a comforter to her.

One would have supposed that the pain of parting from Mr. Earnscliffe could hardly have been surpassed, for to Flora indeed

> " Light was but where he look'd—life where he moved."

Yet time had developed still greater degrees of suffering than that which the mere separation from him caused her to endure.

As soon as they returned to Ireland, Flora devoted herself to reading works on the authority of the Church, and as much as possible avoided going into society. Had she been of a pious and passive temperament, she would naturally have had recourse to prayer, and to what are called

the consolations of religion, in her great trial;
but, unfortunately for her, she could find no solace
in these, and reading such books as we have
named was the only thing in which her restless,
tortured spirit found even momentary rest. It
seemed as if she had a craving for whatever could
strengthen her still more in the conviction that
the great principle of supernatural truth had
positively demanded the tremendous sacrifice
which she had made. Sometimes, indeed, when
she saw her mother looking unusually unhappy
about her she would try to rouse herself, and go
about among their friends, but she quickly
flagged again, and returned to the one absorbing
study.

Thus the summer and autumn passed away, and
November—with its short, gloomy days, and grey,
foggy atmosphere—had set in, when one day, as
Flora was looking over a list of new books, her
hand suddenly trembled, and the paper almost
fell from it, but she caught it in the other hand,
and, with eager eyes, read over and over again to
herself one title which appeared to grow until it
covered the whole list, and she could see only it.
That title was, "THE CATHOLIC CHURCH: ITS
TEACHINGS AND ITS INFLUENCE UPON THE HUMAN
HEART AND MIND," by Edwin Earnscliffe.

"My child! what is the matter? You look so

frightened!" exclaimed Mrs. Adair who was
sitting opposite to her.

"Write for it, mamma," was Flora's answer,
as she handed her the list, and pointed to Mr.
Earnscliffe's name. "I —— something or other
makes my hand shake to-day, so I would rather
not write myself."

"It is better for you not to get it, dearest—it
can only give you pain."

"Mamma, not read *his* book! I *must* read it
whatever it is. I can guess but too well what its
spirit must be ; but, believe me, it is better that
I should *know* its contents than that my imagination should picture them to me. Mamma, it
would be cruel to wish to keep *his* book from me."

"My poor child! I only meant to spare you
more suffering, and therefore it is that I would
rather not get that book for you."

"Yes, I know ; but, as I said, to refuse it to
me will only add to my suffering. Write,
mamma, please to write!" And Flora stood up,
got a writing-book, and placed it before her
mother; then she knelt down beside her, and
again said in a low, pleading tone, "Write."

"I cannot refuse you, darling," replied Mrs.
Adair, "yet to read that book will only foster
sad memories which you must forget if you are
ever to have peace of mind again. Would I

could teach you to forget!" Mrs. Adair sighed deeply, and laid her hand on Flora's head.

" It would be as easy to teach the ivy to detach itself from the oak round which it twines, as to teach me to forget," rejoined Flora slowly, as she looked up earnestly at her mother.

Again Mrs. Adair sighed as she silently took the pen and wrote the desired order.

The book arrived from London by return of post, and Flora eagerly seized it, and carried it off to her room.

It possessed the almost irresistible fascination which such works always do possess when they appeal at the same time to the head and heart, and are written with the true eloquence flowing from " *une âme passionnée.*" The eloquence of this book, however, flowed, alas! from the soul of one who, blinded by pride and passion, had turned away from Light, and devoted his grand powers to the advocacy of darkness, but who cast upon the darkness a halo of seeming truth and beauty. Over those pages, indeed, might angels have wept to see so much that was good and great perverted to evil.

Flora read that book in trembling, yet week after week she spent studying it almost line by line, until she must nearly have known it by heart. She would not, however, let even her mother read it, and when alone she would exclaim aloud, "It is too terrible to think that this is my work! It is as he himself said, 'You found me bereft of hope, but a calm fatalist; you send me from you a blasphemer!' When he was a calm fatalist he dragged none others down with him, but now that he has written this book, how many will be carried away by the powerful eloquence—gloomy and mysterious though it be—of his apparently profound reasoning! He will be responsible for the ruin of all those souls, but it is I who shall have made him become the cause of their ruin! O God! can he have been right when he said, 'It cannot be the voice of Truth or Charity which tells you that you ought to drive to desperation the wounded heart which you had won and promised to heal, rather than infringe a mere regulation of your Church?'"

Then would ensue a fierce struggle between the great contending powers of Faith and unbelief; but her constant study of Truth during the last few months now came to her aid, and gradually she would become calm again, remembering what she herself had so often said to her lover, namely, that the principle of obedience to a revealed and an unerring source of truth upon earth, must be maintained at any cost, or else the mysteries of life and death, of good and evil, would be irreconcilable with the existence of a beneficent Creator, and then life with its tremendous sufferings would be nothing short of a curse.

The cup of human misery seemed now to be filled to the very brim for Flora, and yet it was not; the last drop had to be added still, and the most bitter of all, for it was added by him whom she so loved, and that too when it depended on his own will alone to save her from any farther trouble. How true it is that the sufferings inflicted upon us by our fellow-creatures are almost always more difficult to bear than those which God sends us direct from His own hand!

A few days before Christmas Mina Blake went to see Flora, and after the usual greetings were over she said, " Poor Flora, how pale and tired you look; but I think I know something that will bring the roses back to your cheeks and the light to your eyes."

" Ah, Mina! you cannot know anything that would call the dead to life again ; my roses and brightness, are buried for ever."

" Not so, Flora. . . . Would not the roses bloom and the eyes sparkle again, if the sun of former days could shine upon them once more ?"

" Mina ! " exclaimed Flora, almost indignantly, " how can you trifle so cruelly with me ? "

"I am not trifling, Flora; the same sun in whose light you once so loved to bask is now free to shine upon you with greater brilliancy than ever, and the one dark obstacle to your full enjoyment of it is removed. Flora, Mrs. Stanly, alias Mrs. Earnscliffe, is no more!"

⸗ How unspeakable is the delight of having the portals of hope re-opened when we believed them to be closed to us for ever in this world! Flora uttered a cry of joy, as she heard that they were no longer closed to her; but then she covered up her face in her hands and did not speak again for some moments. At last, however, she said, putting down her hands and showing a face as flushed as it had been pale before, "How do you know it? Mina, tell me quickly, are you certain that it is so?"

"You surely can't suppose that I would have said anything to *you* about it until I knew it beyond all doubt. A week ago I saw the death of a Mrs. Alfred Stanly in the paper, and thought to myself, what joy it would be for you if she were the late Mrs. Earnscliffe; so without a moment's delay I wrote to a cousin of mine in London, to find out who the Mrs. Alfred Stanly —wife to one of the higher officials in the Foreign Office—who was just dead, had been before her marriage to Stanly. My cousin is a very matter-of-fact sort of person, so without many comments upon my curiosity about Mrs. Stanly, he wrote back to me saying that he had made the most particular inquiries about the deceased lady, and that after a little trouble he had succeeded in learning all about her. The 'all' was that she had been a Miss Foster; then the wife of a Mr. Earnscliffe, from whom she was divorced; and finally she became Mrs. Stanly. I received the glad tidings this morning, and, of course, rushed off to tell them to you at once."

Flora's joy, however, was not unmixed with anxiety; and when she was alone, and able to think with comparative calmness, there arose in her heart a timid dread that Mr. Earnscliffe would not value her love now that she was free to give it to him, having once persuaded himself that it was its weakness which had made her give him up. She knew well his proud nature, and how it must have galled him to think that what he called mere prejudice was stronger in her than her love for him; he could not brook not to be first in the heart of one whom he loved.

As these thoughts filled her mind she exclaimed aloud, " God knows that Edwin has been the first sole possessor of my heart! Light —life—everything—he was to me from the time

I first knew him. But how can I prove it to him? The proof he asked for I dared not give, or my love for him would not have been true; and yet this is my crime, in his eyes—to have obeyed God, and loved *him* too well! Oh, Father of mercy, open his eyes,—let him see *how* I have loved him!"

Flora could pray now as she had not done for a long time; she could now plead for re-union with her beloved, without wishing for the death of a fellow-creature; and the star of hope—hope even of earthly happiness—shone again for her, although the more she thought the dimmer grew its rays. Every line of Mr. Earnscliffe's book was replete with concentrated anger against her, or, at least, against what her religion had made her in his sight; but yet through it all there still pierced a glimmer of that bright star of hope.

She had sent Mr. Earnscliffe from her, so now she thought it only right that she should make the first advance towards a reconciliation, and therefore she wrote to him as follows:—

" Your wife is dead, Edwin, and now, indeed, am I free to devote myself to you, if you will accept my devotion. You are unhappy. Your book tells it to me, even if my own heart had not made me feel it ever since we parted. Let me then try to banish that unhappiness. Let me

heal the wounds that obedience to heaven forced
me to inflict upon you!

"As fondly as I loved you when we stood
together at Achensee, do I love you still—or,
rather, far deeper is my love now, for it has been
tested by the fierce fire of sacrifice."

She did not know where he was, so she begged
Mina Blake to enclose it to his bankers in London,
with a request that it might be forwarded to him
at once.   When this was done, she thought to
herself, " If he rejects me now, the last and
sharpest point will have been placed in my thorny
crown ; but, O God, let my misery at least win
for him eternal light and life!"

For a time after this letter had been sent off,
Flora looked brighter and happier.   But it was
like the light before death ; for when a full month
had passed and no answer came, she fell into a
state of despondency far more dark and gloomy
than that which preceeded this momentary
brightening.

In her mother's presence she did her best to
hide the despair which was gathering round her
heart.   But in vain she tried to apply herself to
any occupation.   The only thing that seemed to
please her was to take long, solitary walks into
the country ; and every day, wet or dry, she went
out for at least two or three hours, until at

last she caught a heavy, feverish cold, and was obliged to keep her room for a week. But when she was able to go about again her love of walking had given place to a feeling of unconquerable lassitude; and she never expressed any wish save to be allowed to lie on the sofa. The illness of a cold was gone, but the cough remained, and the doctor talked about the necessity of rousing and amusing her. How this was to be done, was the question upon which poor Mrs. Adair daily and hourly pondered, as she watched with aching eyes her darling growing pale and thin. Mina Blake was unremitting in her attentions to her friend; driving out with her, sitting with her, talking to her, and trying by every means in her power to interest Flora in the present, and prevent her from dwelling so much on the past. But her success was not in proportion to her exertions, and she saw that unless Flora could be roused into interesting herself about something or other, there was no hope of saving her from falling into a gradual decline.

Summer came, but Flora did not regain her strength; and when, in the beginning of June, Lord Barkley so unexpectedly called and earnestly begged to see her, she felt scarcely equal to receiving him; but for Marie's sake she made the effort, and she thought herself richly rewarded when, at the end of a short time, Marie wrote to announce that her happiness was complete, as Colonel de St. Severan had consented that she should be married to Lord Barkley in the following October; and to ask Flora to be her bride's-maid.

Meanwhile Flora's health had not improved; her weakness and languor were slowly but steadily increasing. The doctors looked grave, shook their heads, and suggested the usual resource in such cases—a winter on the Continent —when they find that their skill fails to touch the patient's malady. So when Marie's letter arrived it was decided that they should start at once for Paris, rest there until after the wedding, and then go on to Rome, for Flora expressed so ardent a desire to spend the winter there in preference to any other place, that even the doctors said it was better not to thwart her, although the climate of Rome was not exactly the one which they would have chosen for her.

Rome—Frascati—the birthplace of her love, was most dear to Flora, and in her own heart she thought, "If I could only die in Rome! there where I first saw him, and where I feel certain he will one day bend in homage before the seat of Divine truth living upon earth, then at last he will understand me, and weep tears of love and sorrow over my grave,—tears which will reach me in eternity and make me blest."

Even trials could not make Flora a saint, and instead of praying like Teresa to suffer or to die, or like Mary Magdalen of Pazzi, to suffer and not to die, she prayed for death—for rest from earthly suffering. . . .

CHAPTER XV

ONE Sunday morning in the month of October, two gentlemen were standing in the large room of the Hotel Sirene, at Sorrento, which commands so matchless a view of the beautiful Bay of Naples.

The two gentlemen were Mr. Blake—Mina Blake's uncle—and Mr. Earnscliffe. Although they were not acquainted, Mr. Blake and his new companion were engaged in an animated conversation on the state of Italy. Whilst they talk together, let us take a short retrospective glance over Mr. Earnscliffe's life since we saw him in Paris.

He carried out his original intention of spending a short time in Germany, and there, wandering from place to place, he traced out the plan of that book which had rendered Flora Adair so doubly unhappy. It was completed at Gottingen during a residence there of some four or five months.

No effort had been spared by him in order to render his reasoning forcible, and his burning indignation against her whom he loved—or, rather, against that religion which had made her what she was to him—lent to it the charm of which we have already spoken, namely, that of appealing to the heart as well as to the mind. Whilst the latter reasoned for him, the former burned with feelings which infused into his writing a passionate earnestness well nigh irresistible.

The title of his book gave a fair idea of its tendency. It sought to prove the destructive effect of an institution which claimed for itself unerring authority in its teaching, and demanded unquestioning obedience thereto. "Were it needful to recognise such an authority," he asked, " of what use would reason be to man ? "

Dryden could have told him, had he chosen to be taught, that

> " Dim as the borrow'd beams of moon and stars
> To lonely, weary, wandering travellers,
> Is reason to the soul : and as on high
> Those rolling fires discover but the sky,
> Not light us here ; so reason's glimmering ray
> Was lent, not to assure our doubtful way,
> But guide us upward to a better day.
> And as those mighty tapers disappear
> When day's bright lord ascends our hemisphere,
> So pale grows reason at religion's sight,
> So dies and so dissolves in supernatural light."

But he listened only to the promptings of his

proud will, and strove to deny the Divine light enlightening the world by authoritative teaching.

He was too well schooled a thinker not to know that the fact of a formal divine revelation being once recognised it naturally followed that it should be transmitted in an unerring manner, and not be left to the changeableness of human opinion. He struck, therefore, directly at the basis of all positive revelation by endeavouring to show that the only authority which claimed to speak exclusively in the name of God, sacrificed to its own thirst for domination all the best and highest powers of mankind. In thus losing sight of the distinction between what is human and what is divine in religion—branding St. Peter as an unworthy teacher because he was "a sinful man"—and therewith of the holy precepts of charity, he condemned alike God and man, by seeking the divine guide in the human and—without an unerring teacher—unenlightened conscience. In so doing he flattered pride and self-sufficiency—those two great sources of error in the world—and hence he obtained the erring world's applause.

When his book was finished he left Gottingen and crossed the Alps into Italy ; there he joined in the more active struggle between authority and its antagonists. Nevertheless, he was not satisfied with himself, nor could he bring himself entirely to sympathise with the persons and actions of those whose cause he had espoused and so ardently endeavoured to defend.

The image of Flora Adair, moreover, constantly rose up before him, and thinking of her as he had known her in all things, save in her tenacious clinging to her religious faith, he felt her softening influence often stealing upon him. It was a miserable weakness, he would try to persuade himself; and yet it was something which in his inmost heart he loved. It led him always, he saw, to better and more peaceful thoughts; so true is it that " *God is a centre of love towards which the weight of love directs every creature.*"

These, however, were but fugitive and passing thoughts, yet they awakened and kept alive in him that desire for good, that thirst after what is true, which is the ever-blessed fruit of all real love.

At length he yielded to a strange and increasing yearning which he felt to go to Capri. "I shall find there something real," he would often say to himself, "and little Anina's joy will gladden my heart. . . ."

And what is like the joy of a faithful people? In vain do *they* pretend to it who are without faith and hope in the world. The sunny smile, even more than the sunny sky, is the charm which

attracts our less joyous wanderers to the faithful
Italian people. What wonder, then, that Mr.
Earnscliffe found his old love returning with the
happiness which his presence seemed to create
around him in Capri? Anina's joy and that of
her parents, however, was not without some alloy,
since they all saw with pain his altered appearance, and his habitual expression sterner even
than of old.

His affection for Anina seemed unchanged, and
notwithstanding his more silent and reserved
general manner, he liked to have her with him as
much as ever, although he did not laugh and talk
with her as he had formerly done. One day she
timidly asked him if he were ill, "because," she
said, "he looked so sad and grave now?"

"No," he answered, "I am not ill, *carina;* but
some one whom I loved dearly has made me very
unhappy."

"How wicked it is of any one to make *il caro
Signore* unhappy!" exclaimed the child. "But
I will ask the Madonna to pray that he may be
happy again!"

"Never name the Madonna to me again,
Anina," said Mr. Earnscliffe with a dark frown,
"if you do not wish to offend me!"

The child wondered greatly as to what he
meant by this, and for a long time did not ven-

ture to disobey the command, but all the more did she implore her loved Madonna to pray for his happiness.

During his quiet sojourn at Capri, Mr. Earnscliffe heard of his wife's death, and there, too, he received Flora's letter. His pride took fire even at the trustful love which she had shown to him. It was too much for him to receive with the meekness and thankfulness which it deserved, and so by turns he battled with and yielded to the sweet delight which it foreshadowed to him, as it recalled all the happiness which her confiding affection had given him from the well remembered evening at Achensee to that of the fatal ball in Paris.

As our hero's struggle with himself continued and his egotism was from time to time overcome, a soft light would steal into his eyes, and he would stretch out his arms longing to clasp Flora to his heart again and for ever; but that brightening —like the lightning's flash across a stormy sky —was gone almost as soon as seen, and left behind it only darkness. One day, with a look of proud despair, he turned away his head from the letter which lay before him, and muttered—" No, no! I am not so love-sick as to trust again to one who was so ready to sacrifice me to a senseless regulation of what she calls religion! Flora Adair, you *shall* be torn from my heart whatever it may cost me!"

He seized the letter and crushed it in his hand. After a few moments of seeming thought, however, he threw it, all crushed as it was, into a corner of his desk, and locked it up. Like Count Azo, he was now, indeed, bearing within him "a heart which *would* not yield nor *could* forget."

There were times when evidences of the heroic trust produced by the religion in which Flora Adair believed, crowded before his mind. These testimonies Mr. Earnscliffe had seen in the Catacombs, in history, in the world around him, and, lastly, in Flora's sacrifice of happiness to principle. But pride chased even these away, and his unbending will again and again perverted his better but weaker judgment. "It is impossible!" he would exclaim, "that I have been mistaken after all these years of thought and study! No! I see what this is : it is a weak clinging to a woman whose prejudice is stronger than her love ; but I *will* not yield to it! She shall know that I have sufficient strength to bear wretchedness and loneliness even rather than accept the second place in her heart!" Yet the thought of that letter lying crushed in the corner of his desk haunted him. He longed to look upon her writing again—to read once more all those fond expressions of her constancy ; for he was forced to admit that, at least, she had been *constant ;* but he refused himself even that gratification.

In this turmoil of his heart and mind Mr. Earnscliffe became a more ardent partisan than ever of Italian independence, and we find him at Sorrento, after an interview which he had come there to seek with one of the leaders of that party on the previous Friday. He was about to return to Capri, and even as he spoke with Mr. Blake he was expecting the arrival of Paolo and Anina, as he had promised the latter that she should accompany *il babbo* whenever he came to fetch him home. In mixing himself up with all this party spirit, Mr. Earnscliffe's will had betrayed his judgment into a contradiction of his former respect for things established, his veneration for time-honoured institutions, and the wisdom which experience had tested.

It was an endeavour to justify his new opinions to himself, and to quiet the misgivings which he now so often felt, that had led him to the conversation in which we now find him engaged.

Having reasoned in his book against the existence of any Divine law promulgated in mankind by a living authority, he was endeavouring to persuade Mr. Blake—and perhaps himself—that opinion, or, as he sometimes more speciously called it, conviction and conscience, being the only guide in matters of Divine government, by a stronger reason it was the only authority in human things, and that, therefore, "the voice of the people *is* the voice of God." So far had he already, by the revolt of his will, drifted and well nigh stranded upon the quicksands of revolution!

Mr. Blake was not a yielding listener; he was an older man than Mr. Earnscliffe, and one of those who distrusted the modern notions of progress and liberty; moreover, he did not believe that the same government is good for different peoples, and in his estimate of such things he took large account of "the age and body" of the nations governed. He had read de Maistre, and was strongly inclined to think with him that "*Toute nation a le gouvernement qu'elle mérite.*" He disapproved of the Italian revolution, not in a religious, but in a political point of view, and as the work of foreigners. It shocked his conservative mind to see the uprooting of so much that time had honoured, and principles, rights, and duties treated as if they were things of nought.

"I do not like your revolutionary men," he continued, "much better than their opinions. I find them for the most part gain-seekers for themselves and their followers. It is the result of egotism in all time, and to me a pretty sure sign of wrong-doing. I am not of the Pope's religion, although but a century ago my ancestors were, and there is much in it that I cannot comprehend; but it has *one* charm for me which I confess is great—those who espouse this cause in general are thoughtful and steadfast, ever ready to make any sacrifice for their principles. It is a great test, and a great proof of sincerity."

"Sacrifice! You call it sacrifice? Why, surely their's is the worst of all bondage, the enslaving of the heart, the mind, the whole being; and to what? To a system which governed the dark ages, and which our brighter civilisation has outrun,—the resolute enemy of all progress and enlightenment!"

"Whatever the system may be—and it is too great a question to draw hasty conclusions about —the present manner of dealing with it is, to my mind, unwise and unjust, and I must repeat, the men who are acting against it do. not attract me by exhibiting what I consider to be the necessary virtues of true patriotism. We hear much about confiscation, spoliation, and self-interest in this new era, but steadfast adherence to settled principles, and respect for law and order, have become bywords here."

"'The greatest happiness of the greatest number' is the object of all true patriotism; this I

believe to be the object of these men, and therefore I espouse their cause."

"So far so good," replied Mr. Blake; "but
something remains which you all, I think, lose
sight of; add to it, 'for the greatest length of
time,' and then you will surely find strong
motives for the self-sacrifice which I find wanting
in these too-hastily-formed theories. 'The greatest
happiness of the greatest number' is a phrase
easily made use of to express 'the greatest happiness of myself and those who think with me.' It
is the sacrifice of the present to the future, if
necessary, that calls forth true devotedness. Will
your patience permit me to give you a striking
illustration of this, which I was reminded of but
yesterday in a letter from my niece, and which is
still uppermost in my mind? It is of a young
lady who has sacrificed her heart, her earthly
happiness, and, as I greatly fear, even her life, to
this very principle."

"I shall listen to you with pleasure, but do not
expect me to attach much value to *such* sacrifices.
When women take up particular opinions they
cleave to them with far greater obstinacy even
than men. Weakness, you will grant me, is
generally obstinate!"

"There is not much of weakness, as you will
see, in what I am going to tell you:—

" My young friend and a gentleman whom she met abroad fell in love with each other, and, unlike the usually uneven course of true love, all went smoothly until within a fortnight of the celebration of their marriage, when she learned that her lover had been married before, and that his divorced wife was still living. Poor girl! her religion declares that there can be no such thing as divorce, so she had to choose between her faith and the earthly happiness already within her grasp. Well, she was true to her religion, and made the necessary sacrifice of the present for the future life! Her lover left her, as I am told, in great indignation, and she came home to Ireland looking broken-hearted. She rarely visited anywhere; and my niece, an old schoolfellow of hers, was almost her only companion. In what, as I suppose, was a fit of selfish revenge, the man wrote a book, which, it seems, gave her greater pain than all, since she gathered from it that her very steadfastness had been made the cause of his bitter sarcasm against all that she held sacred.

" One day the newspaper announced the death of his wife, and my niece was filled with joy in the hope that her friend's troubles would now be at an end; but no, the gentleman, it appears, was not so constant as she had been : he was now free

to marry, but he did not come back to her. It is
quite painful to watch her calm outward demean-
our, and yet see, what is so evident, that a worm
is in her heart. Poor child! they say she is in a
decline, and the doctors have prescribed for her
that last resource, a winter in the south. I travelled as far as Paris with her and her mother,
and left my niece with them. I could not bear to
take away that pleasure from her. They wait
there for some family event—a marriage—and
then come on to Italy. Now this steadfastness in
what she believes to be true is what I call a car-
dinal virtue, carried to the point of heroism! If
she dies, which is not improbable, it will be very
like martyrdom. What do you think of it?
Judging from the effect to the cause, we can
hardly help venerating a principle which produces such effects. When you can show such in
favour of these modern theories, I may perhaps
be inclined to think better of them; as it is, I
see everywhere a display of selfishness, rather
than this devotedness."

Every word that Mr. Blake uttered fell upon
Mr. Earnscliffe as a bitter reproach and a sharp
punishment. He had no need to ask that heroine's
name,—he knew it almost from the beginning. A
crowd of contending feelings rushed upon him as
Mr. Blake proceeded; at last he murmured to

himself, "And this it is which, in my selfish pride, I have spurned and mistrusted!"

When Mr. Blake ceased speaking, Mr. Earnscliffe, with a sudden start, exclaimed, "Yes, this *is* something to admire; and the cause which produces it in such a creature as Flora Adair must be good! But do not tell me that her health is in real danger, that would be too much!"

"Good heavens, sir! what is all this?" cried Mr. Blake, shocked by the scared expression of Mr. Earnscliffe's face. "Do you, then, know Flora Adair? Is she a relation of yours, that you should be so startled on hearing this news of her?"

"Relation! No, bear with me, my dear sir, I am the unworthy cause of all her suffering!"

"God be praised, then, that I have been led to see you! I have always felt that there must be some misunderstanding in this matter. Cheer up, sir, all may yet be well!"

The door opened, and a waiter came in to say that the boatman, Paolo, was waiting to see *sua Eccellenza.*

Mr. Earnscliffe took Mr. Blake's hand, and pressed it warmly. "I can never repay you for what you have unknowingly done for me! I must leave you now. Shall I find you here to-morrow? At three I will wait for you. Let me

count upon your secresy for the present, and
until to-morrow adieu !"

"*God is a centre of love towards which the
weight of love directs every creature.*" The weight
of love had all but overcome even the unruly
will of Mr. Earnscliffe. How amply would Flora
Adair have been repaid for all her suffering
could she but have seen the power of her love
now working in that proud man's heart! But
love's brightest conquests are unseen, unknown
even, save in that trustful consciousness felt only
by those who truly love. . . .

Having directed that Paolo should wait a
moment for him, Mr. Earnscliffe turned into the
long corridor of the hotel. His heart was too
full, its flood-gates were yielding, the battle with
his pride was nearly won. Was joy or sorrow
uppermost? He hardly knew; yet it was the
forecoming of joy, the dawn of hope outstripping
the darkness of his gloomy night! "Not the
heart only, but the mind also, is drawn by love;"
and, as his *heart* thrilled at the consciousness of
Flora's love, so his *mind*, no longer trammelled
by his haughty will, not only began to recognise
the greatness of her steadfastness under severe
trial, but the justice too of its cause.

Drawn along for a time by this foreshadowing
of coming happiness, he turned at length to him-

self, and saw the obstacle which had before shut out the vision of Flora's heroism to him. That obstacle was himself—his own pride, his selfishness, his uneducated will, "weakened and inclined to evil," as is the common lot of all mankind. Almost overwhelmed with these conflicting emotions, he returned to Paolo and Anina, who were standing outside waiting for him.

As he approached them the child held out her little hand, and said gaily, "Dear signore, now that we are at Sorrento, will you not come and say one little prayer to our Madonna with me? Please me greatly, signore, and come with me before we return!"

Ah! who shall tell all we owe to these little ones! . . . The signore was in no frame of mind to refuse Anina's request; nay, he even felt a secret pleasure in yielding to it. It was a shrine hallowed by that religion which had called forth Flora's great trust in its eternal truth; he knew, too, that *she* had the highest veneration for the Mother of the Saviour of men!

These thoughts were passing in his mind as he suffered the child to lead him along. "And why am I incapable of such heroism?" he asked himself. "Why have I no such trust even in myself? Why have I not her faith? . . . "

They had entered the church, and as they

crossed the threshold Anina let go his hand, and
went and knelt before the statue of the Madonna.
She made the holy sign, and then closed her
hands to pray. . . . "Why am I so little in my
own estimation before this peasant child?" again
thought the signore. "Why can I not be like
her, and pray?"

"*La conversion*," writes Bossuet, "*est une illu-
mination soudaïne.*" It was the Saviour of mankind who said, "Lo! I stand at the door and
knock; if any man will hear my voice, and will
open the door, I will come in and sup with him
and he with me." The door was open—the proud
man had been already led to acknowledge his
insufficiency to himself, to envy even a little
child's simple faith. The rays of grace had
reached his heart, now no longer closed by pride,
and light and heat had entered there together.
A recollection came to him of words read long,
long ago: "Ask and receive, that your joy may
be full." He yielded to the heavenly invitation,
and he, too, fell upon his knees and prayed for
guidance, light, and love! . . .

.   .   .   .   .   .

It has been said that if an insect could pray to
us when we are about to tread upon it, its prayer

would excite in us great compassion. The more lowly the place whence the lamentations of the heart arise, the more certain is the success of its prayer. It was "the *lowliness* of His hand-maiden" which the Lord " regarded," when He " magnified" her whom He declared to be "blessed among women ! "

Mr. Earnscliffe's heart had become humble and meek, and before he returned to Capri with his dear little Anina, *his* " soul," too, had begun "to magnify the Lord, and *his* spirit to rejoice in God *his* Saviour !"

CHAPTER XVI

THE light which had dawned upon Mr. Earnscliffe showed him, indeed, the sanctuary wherein
truth was to be found, but it showed too how
much was required of him before he could be
admitted within its precincts.

He who had passed in judgment the works of
the great sages of old had now to bend to instruction in the simple truths which every
Christian child knows; and he who had never
acknowledged any other judge over his actions
save his own proud will, had now to unfold even
his erring heart's most secret thoughts to the
apparently human tribunal at which he had so
often scoffed.

Nevertheless he quailed not before the ordeal,
nor tried to turn away his eyes from that truthful
—yet to him dreadful—mirror, wherein he saw,
as in a magnifying glass, the greatness of his
erring; the terrible evil which his book might
do in the world, and all the suffering which he

had so cruelly inflicted upon one who loved him with rare devotedness, and to whom, in spite of himself, his heart had ever clung with passionate attachment.

How vividly did the memory of their last interview rise up before him as he remembered Flora's sad prophetic manner, when she said in answer to his bitter reproaches, "It would be fearful to think that such a sacrifice as mine should be made in vain! Truth *must* dawn upon you at last, though I may not live to see that day, and then, Edwin, you *will* do me justice."

His pulse seemed to stand still as he thought of what Mr. Blake had told him—of the more than possibility that her words might be fully verified —that she might die, just as he had learned to know the true beauty and value of the treasure which he had so madly thrown away.

A feverish impatience to see her again took possession of him. "Yet," he thought to himself, "I must not go to her until I can take with me the hard won flag of faith, and· lay it at her feet as the glorious trophy of her heroism. This very day I will go to Père d'Aubin, and ask him to explain what is still dark to me in the faith for which she has so valiantly suffered."

Père d'Aubin, or as the people called him, Padre d'Aubini, was a Frenchman, who, when comparatively a young man, had been forced to leave his country by ill-health, and although he was now quite well again, he made no exertion to get himself removed from Capri.

His venerable appearance and genial manner had often attracted Mr. Earnscliffe's attention. From a few accidental conversations, too, which he had had with him, he knew him to be a man of no mean acquirements, and one who must have seen much of the world in his earlier days. Yet there he was, devoting himself to the spiritual care of poor illiterate peasants, and making it seem that to be with them and to do them good was happiness to him, although deprived of home and friends and all real companionship. Heretofore he had been an enigma to Mr. Earnscliffe, who could not ascribe his devotion to the priesthood, as he habitually did that of others, to ignorance, or desire of self-aggrandisement.

Père d'Aubin might well have been called learned, yet he sought not a field where that learning could have been displayed, and have gained for him power and fame. What then *was* it that rendered him apparently happy in the humble, simple life which he led on this poor island?

This question was one of the many riddles

which by degrees were being solved for Mr.
Earnscliffe; and he felt that he could have no
better guide in the path of truth than Père
d'Aubin.

On arriving at his hotel his first work was to
open his desk, take out Flora's letter which he
had thrust into one of its corners, and press it to
his lips. After a moment or two, however, of
indulgence in old and sweet memories, he said,
"But I must hasten on with the great work
which is before me; then I will go to her and——
and, yes I feel it, she will return me good for
evil; the measure of her love and goodness will
exceed even the measure of my offences."

Great was Père d'Aubin's wonder when his
simple untrained servant burst into his room and
whispered in an important tone, "*Il gran Signor
Inglese.*"

Père d'Aubin, however, rose to receive his
unexpected visitor, with that dignified courtesy of
manner which so characterised him; and his
surprise was soon changed into joy as he learned
why Mr. Earnscliffe had thus sought him. Then
with sincere emotion he bade him be welcome—
thrice welcome, to the home of his eternal Father.

As Père d'Aubin gradually unfolded to him
the science of Christianity, he began to understand the Saviour's words, "*To you it is given to*

*know the mysteries of the Kingdom of Heaven, but to
them only in parables "*—for now indeed he found
the key to all the *living* mysteries which he saw
carried on and perpetuated around him, and
which not all the philosophers of ancient or
modern times had ever been able to explain to him.

It would be vain to say that *all* his difficulties
were over now—that the ascent from doubt and
negation to the portals of *super*natural truth was
henceforth plain and easy.   On the contrary,
every step on that upward road required a new
effort—an effort made too at the cost of some
old feeling or preconceived idea which early
association and habit had rendered dear and
familiar.   But Mr. Earnscliffe did not want
for courage, and his will being now submissive,
he was able to recognise the proofs which he had
hitherto *chosen* to ignore,—so bravely he fought
" the good fight."

It was only after a conference of several hours
that he left Père d'Aubin, but during that time
the great victory had been gained, although he
felt that there were many points upon which he
still required much instruction.   Yet the time was
very short, as he was anxious to be able to sail
for Marseilles without delay.

Accordingly he again sought Père d'Aubin at
an early hour the next morning, and remained with

him until he was obliged to go in order to keep
his appointment with Mr. Blake.

With emotion, such as perhaps few men can
ever feel, was Mr. Earnscliffe's heart brimming
over as he entered Mr. Blake's room and related
the effect which his conversation of yesterday had
had upon him. How it had all at once illumined his
mind and brought about his seemingly sudden conversion,—" only *seemingly* sudden," he continued,
" for it was but the full development of thoughts
and feelings which have for a long time been
knocking at my heart, but to which I, in my
great pride, deemed it weakness to listen. Once
more I thank you for having made me see myself
as I am, and for having thus helped to break
down the barriers which separated me from truth
and happiness. Now, perhaps, Flora may yet
be mine."

Mr. Blake's good-natured interest in the happiness of his niece's friend prevailed over his
natural feelings of annoyance upon being told
that he himself had been instrumental in this
work, and he exclaimed heartily, " Upon my soul,
I can't be very sorry for this, though of course I
think you are deluding yourself sadly in going so
far. It will be such joy, however, to that poor
girl that it would be almost cruel to her to try
and convince you of the extravagance of your

present feelings. I suppose you intend to start for Paris immediately."

"Yes, I go by the direct service to Marseilles to-morrow evening. My object in coming here to-day was twofold: to thank you for the priceless good which you have done me, and to ask you where the Adairs are staying in Paris. I would ask you too for more information about *her* health, only that I dread to hear unfavourable answers."

"And much better not to ask me, my dear sir, as I could only tell you what the medical advisers say,—and it is quite plain that they cannot do much for her; but I have little doubt that you will prove a far more efficient doctor in *her* case than any of them, and under your care I dare say all the bad symptoms will gradually disappear. I have not told you, however, where they are staying,—at the Hotel de Douvres, Rue de la Paix. They are waiting for the marriage of a Mademoiselle Arbi with a countryman of ours—Lord Barkley. It will take place, I believe, the end of next week."

"Ah! so little Marie Arbi is going to be married! She was to have been Flora's bride's-maid,—now I suppose it will be the other way. But I must not think of all that now. I shall be in Paris before then at all events; and God grant that it may be as you say, that I who have caused Flora's illness may have the power to cure it!"

Mr. Earnscliffe buried his face in his hands and remained silent for a few minutes; then standing up, he said in a husky voice, "Mr. Blake, you see how unfitted I am for any companionship save that of my own thoughts. To-morrow morning I am to be received into the Church; I suppose I must not ask you to be present at *such* a ceremony, but I will pray for you then as for one of my greatest benefactors. I may depend upon you, I am sure, not to name me even when you write to your niece; and now good-bye, and may God bless and reward you!"

They pressed each other's hands silently, for neither felt inclined to speak. Great agitation affects even unconcerned bystanders, so Mr. Blake could not witness unmoved that of Mr. Earnscliffe.

There are in the lives of some persons such thrilling extremes of joy and sorrow that it is difficult to write of them without appearing to use extravagant language. One of these extremes Mr. Earnscliffe felt as he repaired on the following morning to the little church of Capri, to enter fully into the communion of the faithful.

In the humble, unpretending sanctuary, adorned

only by the natural flowers with which the loving hands of Maria and Anina had decked it, knelt the once proud, scoffing Earnscliffe. Behind him were "poor, ignorant" Italians; but before him, on the altar steps, stood the priest of God, who, having administered to him the sacraments of Baptism and. Penance, was now about to admit him to the Divine Feast which our heavenly Father bade *His servants* to prepare for His children on their return home. To portray worthily even the outward features of the scene in that little church would require the pencil of a Beato Angelico.

"The joy of a faithful people" could now indeed be seen sparkling in the expressive countenances of the humble witnesses of this august ceremony; and at its close there was scarcely a dry eye in the whole church. Almost immediately after it was over Père d'Aubin was obliged to hurry Mr. Earnscliffe into the sacristy in order to save him from their tumultuous congratulations; and as the good *père* pressed him in his fatherly arms, and called upon God to bless him with all good gifts, Mr. Earnscliffe fairly sobbed like a child.

A gentle knock was heard at the door: Père d'Aubin opened it, and there stood Anina, trembling with eagerness to see her dear *Signore*, and carrying in her hand the little statue of the Madonna which he had given her long ago.

Père d'Aubin looked round at Mr. Earnscliffe to see if he wished that she should be admitted, but he said aloud, " *Vieni figlia mia*,—my little guardian angel, I do believe, who gained for me the blessed *Madonna's* intercession!"

Anina sprang into his arms, saying, " You see, Signore, I have brought her statue with me, because now I know you will not be sorry that you gave it to me."

" Sorry! Ah, no!" he exclaimed, as he reverently took the statue from her and placed it on the table.

A feast had been prepared in the garden of the priest's house for the poor people; but Anina said that they were all waiting to see the signore before they would begin the repast; " And will the Signore not come?" she added, pleadingly.

" Yes, *carina*," he answered, "but I can only stay a moment, as I must start for Naples immediately. You remember, little one, that I told you I should be obliged to go, but I will come back very soon, and, I hope, bring with me a lady whom you must love even better than you love me."

The child shook her little head at this, and gently drew the signore towards the garden.

Père de Aubin accompanied them in compliance with a look from Mr. Earnscliffe, which meant "Come with us, for I depend upon you to get me away quickly."

Accordingly he and Père d'Aubin soon left the good Italians to their feasting, and walked slowly back to the hotel.

As Mr. Earnscliffe received his spiritual father's parting benediction, he murmured, "Pray that all may be well with Flora, and she will know how to thank you for what you have been to me."

.   .   .   .   .

Marie's marriage was celebrated some days earlier than had been originally intended, in order that the Adairs might be free to leave Paris as soon as possible.

At nine o'clock on the morning of Saturday, the 15th of October, the wedding party assembled in the Church of St. Thomas d'Aquin. The little bride looked pale, but charmingly pretty, in her long flowing dress of rich white satin, and veil of delicate lace, which descended nearly to her feet.

Near her stood her first bride's-maid, Flora Adair. She too was pale, but, unlike Marie, no joyous light beamed from her eyes to redeem that paleness; and, as the ceremony proceeded, it seemed only to increase.

At the close of the Mass, and as Lord Barkley led his now blushing bride down the aisle, Flora whispered to Colonel de St. Severan, "Will you take mamma and Mina in your carriage, and let me return to the hotel. I do not feel strong enough to be at the breakfast, but if I can I will see Marie before she goes away. I must tell mamma, and then, I hope, you will help me to get home quietly."

Colonel de St. Severan made some remonstrance, but a s Flora—after saying a few words to her mother—looked up in his face, he saw that she was scarcely able to stand, and quickly drawing her hand within his arm, he took her at once to the carriage, and desired Marie's maid to go with her to the hotel.

When they arrived there, Flora thanked the maid for having left the gay scene to accompany her, desired the coachman to drive her back, and slowly went upstairs.

That wedding had been, indeed, too much for her. She only just reached the sofa in time to save herself from falling; feebly she loosened the strings of her light tulle bonnet, and let it drop unheeded upon the floor, and murmured, "Edwin! if I could only see you once more, and you would believe in me, I should die happy! But perhaps he has ceased to be angry with me—ceased even to think of me! Yet no, he is not one likely to forget; it was not forgetfulness that made him so cruel as not even to acknowledge the receipt of my letter. Ah! how differently he felt when he gave me this!"

Flora took from the little table beside her a beautifully bound and illustrated edition of Schiller's "William Tell," and sought out that scene between Rudenz and Bertha, the opening lines of which were so imprinted on her heart that she needed not a book to recall them to her memory; yet she loved to read them over and over again, out of *his* present, and dream of the happy evening when he spoke them to her.

To-day, however, as she came to the last line, she burst into a fit of sobbing, and the page became wet with her tears. At length, exhausted by her own emotion, she fell asleep. . . .

Meanwhile, Mr. Earnscliffe had travelled post-haste, or rather steam-haste, from Naples. He reached Marseilles late on Thursday evening, and the following night he took possession of his old Paris quarters, in the Rue Castiglione—the Hotel de Londres.

That night seemed to him an eternity—an eternity which separated him from the object of all his hopes. Vainly he tried to still the beating of his heart, so as to consider *calmly* what he should do in the morning. Should he go at once to Mrs. Adair, or should he write to her?

But neither of these plans pleased him,—he could not think of anything to say or to write to Mrs. Adair, nor indeed of aught save Flora herself; and thinking of her put every other thought to flight, for it conjured up visions which made him feel hot and cold by turns, as they varied from bright to dark and dark to bright.

Thus the night dragged through, and morning found him still more feverish and incapable of forming any definite idea of how he was to get over the interview with Mrs. Adair. He had quite discarded the idea of writing—and knew not how to reach Flora's presence; but see *her* he must, and as soon as possible, for he could bear this suspense no longer.

He, of course, knew nothing of the change about Marie's wedding, and naturally supposed that the Adairs would certainly be at home about ten in the morning. Much after this his impatience would not permit him to wait.

The distance from the Rue Castiglione to the Rue de la Paix was so short that Mr. Earnscliffe preferred to walk; he hoped, besides, that the air and exercise would tend to calm him, yet it was in a hardly steady voice that he asked at the Hotel de Douvres for Madame Adair.

The concierge looked to see if the key was in its appointed place, and not seeing it, he answered the question in the affirmative, and indicated the *étage* and number of their apartment.

Tremblingly Mr. Earnscliffe knocked at the door, but he heard no answer. Again he knocked, —still no answer. Could the concierge have been mistaken about their being at home? They might have gone out and have taken the key with them.

A sickening feeling of disappointment crept over him, and he was moving away, when it occurred to him that this door might only be an outer one, and that consequently his knocking might not have been heard, even if they were at home.

He went back and turned the handle. It *was* an outer door, and closing it behind him, he advanced to an inner one which was partly open.

The sight which that half-open door disclosed to his view arrested his steps on the very threshold, and he stood for a moment like one transfixed.

There was Flora, ·in that strange, half-bridal costume, stretched upon the sofa, seemingly almost lifeless. Those closed eyes—that pallor—

what did it all mean?   And striking his forehead with his clenched hand he murmured, " O
God, make not my punishment greater than I
can bear ! "

Then stealing softly over to the sofa he knelt
down beside her and listened with rapture to the
low sound of her breathing, even whilst he
marked the hectic appearance of her complexion ;
and well he remembered how different it was
formerly!

He tried to keep himself quiet in order not to
disturb her, but as he looked at the little thin
hand, resting upon the open book as if pointing
even in sleep to those words of Rudenz', he could
not resist the temptation to touch it with his lips.

Even sleep could not deaden Flora's sense of
that electric touch ; she started up, and gazing at
him as one risen from the dead, cried, " Edwin ! "

He, too, sprang to his feet, held open his arms,
and forgetting all his intended prayers for
pardon, he merely exclaimed, " My ever loved
one ! your words have come true—your sacrifice
has won for me the light of Divine truth, and at
last I do you justice ! Flora, will you come to
me now? "

To her, his presence, his words, were like the
rays of a fierce sun, which darted in at her eyes,
at her ears, and piercing to her very brain,

made her reel with delight, and she sank insensible into his arms.

We have all read the fable of the statue into which life was infused by the strength of the sculptor's passion. Thus did the ancients symbolise the power of love. May we not then justly infer that Flora did not remain very long insensible in Mr. Earnscliffe's arms! And afterwards, as she listened to his recital of the dawning and progress of that supernatural light which now shone upon him, and recognised throughout her own influence in leading him to it, full indeed was her cup of happiness—happiness such as she could never have known had she not purchased it so dearly! . . .

.   .   .   .   .   .

To live in the enjoyment of fame and honour is not necessarily the reward of a brave soldier, and how often is the bravest cut down in the full flush of victory! When perhaps he has achieved some glorious deed, and is revelling in the proud consciousness of having served his country, the fatal blow falls, and with a last struggle he yields up the life which had just become so doubly dear to him.

Even so is it with the bravest soldiers in the

great battle of life itself. The joys of earth were not the especial reward promised to them, and as they too are revelling in delight over some victory, so great that they had not dared to look forward to its achievement upon earth, they are often called upon to relinquish the sweet human happiness already within their grasp. It is the final test of courage and sacrifice which the Divine Commander asks at their hands, in order to crown all their past brave deeds, and entitle them to a still higher place in the realms of unfading glory and bliss, where the souls of those who have *truly* loved here below will be united, to part no more, but to endure for ever in God. . . . Such a triumph of the spirit over the flesh is great indeed, but oh! how painful to our poor weak human nature! Therefore we will not stay to witness it, but will bid Flora Adair and Edwin Earnscliffe good-bye in their short hour of ineffable happiness.

THE END.